T0157795

JONATHAN C. AKIN

Now Entering Obscurity

iUniverse, Inc.
Bloomington

iUniverse books may be ordered through booksellers or by contacting:

iUniverse
1663 Liberty Drive
Bloomington, IN 47403
www.iuniverse.com
1-800-Authors (1-800-288-4677)

ISBN: 978-1-4620-0438-6 (sc)
ISBN: 978-1-4620-0439-3 (ebook)

Printed in the United States of America

iUniverse rev. date: 03/18/2011

To my friends,
Tim Howard and Debbie Rose

Other novels by Jonathan C. Akin

Interrations

Winner's Choice

Acknowledgments

I'd like to thank the following for their help beyond just their daily support and encouragement and the sharing of their lives and friendships: Tim Howard; You always seem to know where I should direct my focus, Melba Gross; You are just the best darn P.R. person anyone could hope for, Robert Chambers; You didn't spill the beans to anyone, Debbie Rose; You read and gave me feedback on the first half (and the fact that you've read my other two novels so many times) and kept me going while waiting so patiently, Mom; You kept me from having to think about all those other things, Dad; Your keen eye kept me true to my words, Mark and Shannon Massaro; You two, in addition to so many other things, introduced me to a new attitude, Tammy Mansfield; You trusted me with your soul, Darlene Popplewell; You know when to stand by me and when to jump out of the way, Victoria Pichardo; You are my cultural epicenter, Daniel Murphree; You re-entered my life (albeit too briefly) at just the right time, Alana Edwards; You shared in the joy of the life of and the mourning of the loss of an old friend, and Rocky; You…well, you are just you, you little goofball.

Now, I have to thank the following for indulging me and allowing me to inundate their lives (plus sharing their lives, friendships, and support and encouragement) for the past few years with what started out as just a way to tell some friends and family what was going on with me and my burgeoning writing career, but has now grown into a monthly e-newsletter reaching twenty-three U.S. states and Canada (and still growing): Candy Abbott, Elyse Aiello-Mann, Charles and Dari Akin, Cheryl and Gary Akin, Jeff and Kate Akin, Jennifer Akin, Sandra Akin, Mike Angeline, Terre AshBrook, Sue and Jim Atzemis, James Avant, Jenny Baer, Barbara Baldwin, Diana Bowman, Jerome Brown, Cheri Calloway, Pam and Brian Campbell, Greg Carter, Pelle Cass, Marcus Causey, Brian DiNapoli, Mary Jo Dinser, Lori Drake, Ann Marie Droluk, Margaret Dyer, Alana Edwards, Cindy Elsberry, Dan Fitzmaurice, Beth Garino, Nilu Gavankar, Cyndi

Gaw, Melissa and J.P. Gegato, Ibrahim Ghanoush, Deborah Gladden, Michael Grogan, Melba Gross, Kelly Grundhoefer, Sherry Hardebeck, Lori Harnist, Barry Harvey, Jim Hasse, Madeline Hatter, Darlene Hauck, Terry Henderson, Tim Howard, Fran Hyc, Prince Johnson, Candace Juergen, Judy Lacina, Denise Leon, Linda Littman, Nikisha Lucier, Bernadette Luebberst, Diana Lynn, Mary Jane Mahan, Tammy Mansfield, Mark and Shannon Massaro, Jonathan Maxwell, Lea Mayes, Maria McGee, Erika McGill, Brooks Mendell, Anara Midgett, Brenda Miller, Tim Miller, Darlene Moeller, Reginald Mullins, Janice Na Pier, Lisa and Andrew Noll, Driana and Sheldon Pearlman, Victoria Pichardo, Darlene Popplewell, Dorethea Powell, Adrianne Ramey, Dominic Rinner, Debbie Rose, Marissa Salas and Wendy Cartier, Janet Schindler, Jenny Schnick, Carol Schott, Stephanie Smith, De'Ron Smith, Shelley Sopczak, Diane and Richard Sopinski, Richard Spaeth, Cindy Stefanini, Betty Tancin, Nancy and Edward Thomas, Caroline Tummino, L. Eugene Vaughn, Linda Waldo, Brad Welage, Amy Whaley, Vernetta Whittaker, Marie Williams, Joe Witham, and Jackie Zuniga-Snell.

Once again, I raise a glass to toast the entire staff of iUniverse, Inc., with extra "clinks" to Ryan Allison, Mara Rockey, Andrea Long, and the London Design Team, and to author Charlotte Turnquist who told me about them.

Last, but certainly not least, I thank you and I hope you enjoy your trip into Obscurity!

Obscurity or Bust

They tell me I'm full of shit. "They" being my friends, Camarada, who I've known since we were freshmen in high school, her girlfriend of eight years, Leslie, and Makker, who I've known for about twelve years since he hired me at his bookstore. Of course I know they tell me this out of love and concern, and Makker and Leslie are a bit more eloquent, but Camarada has always been very blunt.

You see, I suffer from a terminal and debilitating illness and I found out about a year-and-a-half ago what it is called. My doctor, "Dr. Webster", defines it this way; "*noun* (14th century) 1: utter loss of hope, 2: a cause of hopelessness". Okay, my SELF-DIAGNOSED terminal and debilitating illness is "Despair". That's why my friends tell me I'm full of shit.

The onset of my illness happened five years, four months, and eighteen days ago when Lois died. We were together almost fifteen years. We weren't married in the legal and traditional sense, but we said our vows to one another early on. And we both took them seriously. So seriously that, after four years together, we decided to enlarge our family unit.

It took us eight months to find three-year-old Cody. I don't know if Cody fell for Lois first or vice-versa, but it only took about three seconds for her to convince me to sign the papers. That took a little longer, but our family unit was complete. We did change his name to Carlisle, though, just in case there was any residual trauma from his previous owners. Oh, by the way, Carlisle is our...my dog.

Okay, back to my illness and Camarada's, Leslie's, and Makker's "cure" for their diagnosis. Again, Makker and Leslie weren't quite so blunt, but they did more or less agree with Camarada that I just needed to "get laid". They each, in their own way, tried to cure me with potential fix-ups with friends of theirs, approaching strangers that somehow they thought I found attractive, and even registering me on internet singles' sites, to name a few.

For some reason I couldn't convince them that it wasn't that easy. I turned forty-three in the tenth year of the new millennium, hadn't been intimate with, let alone dated, anyone else since I was twenty-two, and, oh yes, there's more, hadn't been intimate with ANYONE since Lois became ill five years before she died. I was like a virgin all over again.

Okay, I have to backtrack a little for a moment to shed a little light on my journey to Obscurity. While Lois was in the midst of her illness, Makker convinced me to start writing the novel that I'd been talking about for a couple of years. The year after Lois died, I finished and published it and, as a matter of fact, I have since written and published a couple of others. I'm nowhere near the likes of Stephen, John, or Eric Jerome, but I make a comfortable living and enjoy my anonymity. I did, anyway.

Sometime soon after my second novel was published, I started receiving correspondence from old girl friends from junior high and high school. The funny thing is they wanted nothing to do with me back then. (I was too safe for them because their parents actually liked me…the kiss of death!) They all wanted the "bad boys" back then. Now, some twenty-five or more years later after they've been done in by the bad boys, they remembered the "nice guy" and finally found me after looking for me for "years and years" as they said. So, with my anonymity going and, of course, having to "lie" around my illness, I yearned for obscurity.

Bringing you back to where I was before I backtracked, I was poking around the internet trying to find someplace to base a novel in and, well, there it was. You guessed it. Obscurity! So, about a year ago, after convincing my friends that I hadn't COMPLETELY lost my mind (I still don't think they believe it, but, oh well), I packed up my car with a couple of bags for me and one for Carlisle and we left for Obscurity. [Note: Not being that spontaneous of a person I did research it for a couple of months before I told Camarada, Leslie, and Makker that I was going away for awhile.]

Anyway, to this day my friends don't know where I and Carlisle are, even though I check in with them regularly on my cell so they know we're still alive, but I did have to tell one person, my agent and manager Aggie Germane, where I was going. Mainly because I needed her to set up credentials, accounts, and such under a false name so I could go live and work (there was a position open at the community college and I figured working would make me less conspicuous) in Obscurity.

Now, I know Aggie hasn't told a soul, but when a forty-(plus)-year-old single man comes to a town that's only big enough to be on a map, the locals get a little curious. Okay, who am I kidding? They get A LOT curious. So, I didn't think it completely through. I blame it on my illness and the effects it has on the mind. Aggie, now that I think about it, did try to tell me this, but I think I told her she was full of shit. I blame that on the Turrets Syndrome that accompanies my illness. That's what I'm going to tell her, anyway.

Okay, as I said, it was almost a year ago that, on the most plain and non-descript day, after driving for about seven hours, I saw a sign. I don't mean a metaphorical or spiritually life-changing sign, but an actual physical and tangible sign. It was on the side of the road and was just as plain and non-descript as the day itself. It read, "Welcome To Obscurity! Enjoy Your Stay!"

Welcome to

OBSCURITY!

Enjoy your stay!

Getting Settled

Lois and I road tripped whenever chance allowed. It's funny that I never thought of it before, but most of our destinations were inspired by television shows and movies. To give you an idea, but not to bore you with the endless list, the Vermont B&B – ala *Newhart*, Graceland – *Designing Women's* Charlene's love of Elvis, and God only knows where (because I sure don't know where we ended up), but we never did find those *Children of the Corn*. We did find corn, though. Holy cob, Batman! Did we find corn!

Anyway, it wasn't until about fifteen minutes after I passed that sign and entered the "Business District" of Obscurity that I realized I was whistling *The Andy Griffith Show* theme and that *Mayberry, RFD* did, in fact, exist. I'd like to say that I laughed at myself, but I actually started whistling louder and waved at the few pedestrians and shopkeepers I saw as I passed them. Okay, don't think that the men were all in suits with skinny ties and the women were in their Sunday best on a Wednesday afternoon, trust me, they weren't. It was, IS, more like "Mayberry, Y2K". [Note to self: VERY interesting title/idea – maybe Aggie can do something with this and it might just get me out of the doghouse with her for telling her she's full of shit.]

So, as I came to the end of the business district, really only two blocks long, I reached over and grabbed for the directions that Aggie had e-mailed me to take me to my "home away from home". I had to go up a somewhat treacherous two lane hillside to what I now know the locals call "The Heights". I was looking for Obscurity Heights and 4523½ Heart Way; an over-the-garage apartment owned and rented out by a fifty-six-year-old widow, Lancome Deladee, whose name I pronounced, at that time, as "de-LAY-dee".

I pulled up to the curb across the street from my new digs and before I could even turn the engine off a more elegant, and much less scary, version of the white-haired *Stop the Insanity!* fitness guru Susan Powter came bounding down the porch of 4523 Heart Way and toward my car. Of course, Carlisle, who had since aroused from his boredom of being captive in the backseat for seven hours except for a few leg stretching and pee breaks along the way, decided to "greet" our new landlady with his impression of *Cujo*.

Quick background of Carlisle: His bark is definitely worse than his bite, not that he's ever bitten anyone, at least, since I've known him. As a matter of fact, Lois and I thought he was mute after we got him home from the pound. He didn't make a sound for four days. Day four is when we could finally get him into a vet for a check-up and that's when he made his first sound as the doctor stuck his gloved finger up his butt. Hey, when my doctor finally tells me that it's time for my first prostate exam, I'll probably yelp, too! By the way, he hasn't really shut up since. Anyway, as vicious as Carlisle can sound, he wouldn't hurt a fly. I'm serious! He's TOTALLY AFRAID of them. If a fly gets into the house, he runs and hides in the bathtub shivering like he's been left outside in Siberia.

Okay, back to Cujo and the landlady. [Note to Aggie: I really don't think there's anything there. Trust me. I've tried.] Anyway, I had turned the engine off and, of course, the windows were down and Carlisle was barking out the window at her. I was totally freaking out and trying to shush him and turn the car back on and put the windows up before she got to us and/or he jumped out and mauled and ate her, but she was too quick.

Now, this is why I instantly and totally fell in love with Lancome Deladee. Not "sexual" love or "love" love, but Respect love, Friend love. She went right up to that back window and put her hands on Carlisle's ears and rubbed them and put her face right up to his and nose-nuzzled him. And do you know what that little shit did? (Carlisle, not Mrs. Deladee.) He plopped his furry little butt down, turned over on his back, and offered his belly to her for, what I could tell was, just THE most exciting belly rub in the history of belly rubs. Sure, it only lasted about fifteen seconds, but if I still smoked and had cigarettes on me, I would've offered him one. Thank God (and Bob Barker) Lois and I had him "fixed".

Okay, so, she un-leaned out of the back window and Carlisle up-righted himself, shook, and then stuck his head out the window and panted heavily as his new friend moved to my window. I hope she didn't notice that I was leaning toward her and hoping for the same greeting. Again, not sexual, but hey, who wouldn't like a good belly rub? And, again, from what I could tell, she knew how to do it!

She said, "Welcome, Mr. Autumns."

I unbuckled my seatbelt and she stepped back as I got out of the car.

I said, "Ryder, Mrs. Deladee, I mean, any friend of Carlisle's is a friend of mine."

She laughed and then corrected me at the pronunciation of her last name. It rhymes with "melody". She then said, "Honey, call me Lana. Everyone does."

Four days later on Sunday night I think I was asleep before my head hit the pillow. Who knew obscurity could be so exhausting? Whoa! Sorry. I jumped ahead. Let me go back.

Okay, after Lana showed me and Carlisle to our new home she let us get settled, that took all of about twenty minutes, then she took us "downtown", the business district, to pick up "a few things" to, as she said, "Masc up the place." Then we masc-ed up the place and then she made dinner and that lasted till about two in the morning as we became kindred spirits as we told each other our life stories, me keeping certain things untold as I "was" incognito.

{Ruth Anne and William Vaughn were both asleep, she in her bed and he in a chair at his wife's bedside, in the semi-private room of Whopping County Hospital when the nurse brought in their newborn baby girl. William awoke first, he hadn't just gone through sixteen hours of labor, and accepted his daughter from the nurse. He sat quietly, mesmerized by the tiny bundle in his arms, until Ruth Anne woke up and asked to hold her.

William sat staring at his wife and daughter, but got up to close the curtains as the bright morning sun broke through the clouds from the storm during the night and came streaming through the windows. Ruth Anne told her husband to leave the curtains open so she could see the tears the angels had wept at the birth of their baby girl streaking the windows. Then she laughed. She saw how the pounding rain had spattered the dirt up from the ground onto the windows and said that the angels cried so much that their mascara had run. They named their daughter Lancome with no middle name.

Lancome Vaughn was Ruth Anne and William's third child, but she grew up alone. Sort of. Her mother had two stillborn baby boys, William Jr. five years before Lancome and the other William Jr. two years after the first. So, even though Lancome was an only child and the two Juniors weren't often mentioned, she did grow up with both of them while being in the "shadows" of their non-existent presence and being closely monitored by her overly protective parents.

Even with the shadows of her "brothers" and the constant monitoring of her parents, Lancome was neither a wild child nor a bookworm and, at sixteen, the raven-haired and porcelain-skinned beauty stood out amongst the nearing ten-thousand residents of Whopping. [Note: In thirty-nine years it's grown to a whopping twelve-thousand-five-hundred, give or take.] She stood out, mostly, to the boys near her age, but, also, to everyone else for her sunny disposition. And there were actually wagers on who would be the young man to win her heart, even though she continuously refused the offers of dates and possible wooing and courting. That's why on a Saturday morning nearing lunch time in downtown Whopping she almost stopped traffic!}

Before I continue, I should let you in on a little secret. I cannot speak for all writers/authors, but in my case I am an A+ student in the courses of Observation and Listening. Everything I'm recounting about my dear friend Lana is what she told me, but I will say that I did not have a tape recorder hidden and different aspects of her life came back up when they were pertinent to our many, many, MANY conversations. The main facts are correct, but I have taken some poetic license for storytelling purposes. What I can promise you is that right before she told me the rest that first night, I was totally transfixed by how her ice-blue eyes sparkled with happiness and glistened with melancholy and how she was completely swept away from the present.

{At the insistence of her parents, Lancome was in downtown Whopping in search of a dress for the Whopping Senior High School Homecoming Dance. Her parents accepted the invitation from Dewey Johnson on her behalf. It's not that she disliked Dewey, he was a nice enough boy and good-looking, or any of the number of other boys who asked her to the dance. It's not that she was outraged by the Vietnam War and thought that the dance was wrong to be held in the midst of all the turmoil. No, she just wasn't interested in going to the dance and she'd just never met anyone who sparked any type of feelings in her. Ever! Until she passed the bus station that day.

She wasn't reading anything or looking in shop windows or looking down at the sidewalk or paying any attention whatsoever to any of the other pedestrian passers-by on the street, she was just in her own world. It was the sound of a bus moving on that brought her attention to a young soldier in his khaki dress uniform standing at parade rest with a duffle bag at his feet. He was just standing there. Looking around. Lost. She still doesn't know why she did what she did.

She knew of the way soldiers were being ostracized when they returned from Vietnam, but that wasn't it. She could tell that he was saddened that even his own family hadn't come to the bus station to greet him home, but that wasn't it. She wasn't necessarily attracted to men in uniform, handsome or not, so that wasn't it, either. All she knows is that she felt something inside pulling her to this young soldier. This STRANGER! She walked right up to him and said, "Welcome home." And then, even at five-feet-ten-inches tall, she stood on her tiptoes as she put her arms around him and kissed him full on the lips. The following Saturday, while Dewey Johnson and the rest of her classmates were enjoying the homecoming dance, she became Mrs. Lawrence Deladee.}

Oh God, I hate to say that I'm a romantic at heart and that her story made me tear up like a baby, but it did. And still does sometimes. I REALLY hate to say it because I'd thought I'd moved on to sarcasm and cynicism! Hey, if you knew me or read my other novels you'd see that I've mastered both.

Anyway, so, Lana doesn't know why her parents let her marry twenty-four-year-old Sgt. Lawrence Deladee when she was only sixteen. She says, always with a laugh, probably because he was the first guy she'd ever shown interest in and they figured they'd better or they'd never get her married off. She doesn't care. They let her and that is all that matters. Anyway, he got a job as a mechanic and they got a small apartment in Whopping. They had their first child, daughter Lisanne, before their first anniversary.

{Lancome found out she was pregnant, again, when Lisanne was only three-months-old. She and Larry weren't poor, he was making decent money because everyone wanted him to work on their cars, but he was very cautious about spending any of their small, but growing, nest-egg and she knew he would try to convince her that their small apartment was big enough for them, Lisanne, and another baby. But she'd had her eye on a modest-sized "fixer-upper" and something else on the outskirts of neighboring town Obscurity for a while. She just needed a plan.

She knew her husband was too proud to take any money from her parents and honestly didn't know if any bank would give them a loan for a house and a business with Larry only being a twenty-six-year-old mechanic with a wife and child and one on the way. She decided to talk it over with her parents. The next day, on Larry's lunch break, she took him to Obscurity to show him a house and "garage". She spent the next week "casually" mentioning to him about trying to get a loan. At the end of that week, she told him that she'd just found out she was pregnant, again. It took her two more weeks to finally get him to go to the bank and apply for the loan. He did it, if for no other reason than to "shut her up". [Note: Those were her words, not his.]}

Okay, let me wrap this up with the *Reader's Digest* version. Larry got the loan. Lana still says, "Thank you, Daddy." They bought the house and "Deladee's Garage". Lawrence Jr. was born. In the next five years there were four more babies; Lucas, Lucille, Deladee's Garage – Whopping, and Deladee's Garage – South Whopping. Fifteen more years and four more "Deladee's Automobile Repair" shops, one in downtown Obscurity and three in neighboring Gross County, the tri-city county consisting of Gross Springs, Shrewesburg, and Green Haven, on the opposite side of Whopping than Obscurity, with the slogan "A shop near you to take care of all of your automobile needs". Eight years later, Lana and Lawrence Jr. convinced Lawrence Sr. to retire and enjoy the rewards of what he'd worked for his entire life and Lawrence Jr. took over the "Deladee Empire".

So, let me catch you up to present day on Lawrence Sr. and the Deladee children. Lana and Larry enjoyed retirement by first buying a home in the new community of Obscurity Heights, decorating it for a year, and then traveling abroad for the next four years until Larry suffered a fatal heart attack in Brussels. Lisanne met her husband, John Bell, while attending Shrewesburg University to get her teaching degree; where they now teach and live with their three children; Ruth, Joseph, and David. Lawrence Jr. sold the family business three years after he took over and is now the Southwestern Regional Vice-President of the company he sold it to (he never married, but has quite the "little black book"). Lucas, never feeling capable of measuring up to his older brother, lives in Whopping and coasts through life going from job to job and girlfriend to girlfriend. Lucille, having always wanted to travel, became a flight attendant and after the airline she worked for for several years folded, she was able to get a job with another airline, Omni Airlines, but on her very first assignment a couple of years ago - Flight 1010 from St. Louis to Cincinnati - the plane met with disaster and she didn't survive.

Wow, did I get side-tracked! I started telling you why I think I was asleep before my head hit the pillow after four days in Obscurity. Well, that was my first day, Wednesday. Thursday was "The Grand Tour" and believe it or not it took all day and I think I learned everything about all one-thousand-seven-hundred-and-fifty-four other Obscurity residents from Lana. Friday, she and I journeyed to Whopping to the community college where I would be teaching. Of course, we had to take the long scenic route there (I learned going back to Obscurity that it was the "only" route) and since we were in "the big city" we had to do lunch and shop and then back home and she made dinner for us, again, another late night. Saturday was some sort of festival downtown (I'm not at all full of myself, but I still believe it was to introduce me to Obscurity) and I think I met all, but one (and that's because she was away at the time taking care of a sick relative), of the seventeen-hundred-and-fifty-four other residents. Oh yeah, Lana made sure that I knew the faces that went with the names and stories she informed me of, for "my benefit", two days earlier. And then Sunday was the morning church service followed by lunch with the pastor and the church board and then the afternoon service followed by dinner with the Mayor, his wife, and a few "select" constituents. Man, I'm tired all over again thinking about it!

Eating Out

Monday morning came and I FINALLY had some time to myself as I set off to Whopping and my first day of Teacher Preparation Week before classes began the following Monday at Whopping Community College where I'd be teaching Creative Writing and, as I found out at the faculty brunch, Public Speaking because neither had huge enrollment and each had been cut down to two classes. Of course, "CW" met on Mondays, Wednesdays, and Fridays, one in the morning and one in the afternoon, and "PS" met on Tuesdays and Thursdays, one in the morning and one in the afternoon, so, I still had to spend all day there every day. [Note to Aggie: I'm not sure if you knew about this and this was payback for my comment, but paybacks for paybacks are even more hellish. Ha-ha!]

So, despite being so exhausted from my first four days in Obscurity I was up early and ready and raring to go. I think Carlisle was still exhausted because all he did after I coerced him into going outside to do his business was jump back up on the bed, sink into the pillows, turn belly up with his legs sticking straight up, and start snoring. He didn't even budge when Lana called me on my cell, which he absolutely HATES the sound of, and asked, quite chipper herself, if I'd be coming down for breakfast before "heading off to school" because "breakfast is the most important meal of the day".

I told her I wouldn't, much to her dismay, and explained that I had a very difficult time eating so soon after getting up and, also, that the "school" was feeding us an early lunch sort of as a "welcome". I did, however, tell her that I'd pick something up on the way home and we'd have dinner together and I'd tell her all about my first day. She accepted "my invitation" of dinner, but said that she'd whip something up. I told her it was a date and she was cheered up.

I, again, coerced Carlisle out of bed because Lana insisted that he keep her company while I was gone until she could have a "doggie door" installed. Now, I'd like to say that I dragged him begrudgingly down to her, but the little shit practically scratched a hole in the door once he heard her name. So, after I "dropped" him off with her I left for school. Yes, I know how silly it sounds for a forty-three-year-old man going off to school, but it makes me feel like I'm eight when I say it and it makes me think of Lana and smile when I say it.

Okay, I have to confess something. I told Lana a little white lie. I WAS feeling quite hungry, but I had already decided after "the festival" on Saturday to grab a bite downtown at The Obscurity Eatery, since I had to pass it, anyway. Okay, there was another reason. I was intrigued by a waitress there. Tatiana Bodaccia. Not romantic intrigue. Don't get me wrong, she's a very beautiful woman with olive skin, straight black hair just down to the middle of her back, curves in all the right places, and (forgive me, ladies) some bodacious tatas. She's, also, my age. Okay, a few years older. Anyway, what intrigued me most about Tatiana was her ethnicity.

Please bear with me for a moment. As I said, I researched Obscurity. One thing I found out is that it is ninety-eight percent White and two percent "Other" races with seventy-five percent of that two percent being Hispanic or Latino. Yes, I did the math. Out of the one-thousand-seven-hundred-and-fifty-five Obscurity residents, one-thousand-seven-hundred-and-twenty are White. That leaves thirty-five residents in the Other category, twenty-six of which are Hispanic/Latino. The nine remaining are African American, Asian, Native American, Other – again, "Other", not quite sure what other there could be – or bi-racial. I'm not going to make any excuses, I completely pushed all thoughts of reasons for the "racial make-up", or lack thereof, out of my mind because I was so longing for obscurity.

Okay, another confession. This is another reason, a very big one, why I've never told Camarada, Leslie, or Makker where I was going. I didn't want them coming to visit and feel uncomfortable. Leslie, at thirty-three and very, very White would fit right in. Well, except maybe for the lesbian part. A "lipstick lesbian", but a lesbian nonetheless. Don't get me wrong, there are homosexuals in Obscurity. Anyway, Camarada, exactly one month older than me, would blend I suppose because she's Mexican (Okay, a little "butch"). And Makker, two years my senior, is African American. VERY dark-skinned African American.

Alright, I'm not that altruistic. There's more. I didn't want to stand out. Don't hate. I love and respect my friends, but sometimes a person's got to do something totally selfish that doesn't make sense to himself or anyone else. And I was YEARNING for obscurity what with my illness. Anyway, I guess that's why Tatiana Bodaccia intrigued me.

{On her eighteenth birthday, Tatiana Zaynab Marguerite Lucinda Oliveros left Puerto Rico and her parents and four sisters for Miami. Life wasn't easy or glamorous, at first, for her in Miami, but it was better than her life in Puerto Rico. The first six months passed rather uneventfully and somewhat grueling, but then she met thirty-seven-year-old Giovanni Paolo Bodaccia and that's when things started to get interesting.}

Before I continue, I guess I should tell you a couple of things. First, Gio's last name, and now Tatiana's, isn't pronounced like the latest fad Italian flatbread, but, and I guess I should do this as phonetically as possible, is pronounced "bo-DAY-shuh". Second, Tatiana less "met" and more "walked in on" Gio at the small dive of a motel that she cleaned rooms at during her day job. See, from what I can put together, one of the desk clerks and the head housekeeper had a little racket going on where they rented out rooms to "quickies" and "less than savory characters" and split and pocketed the money and the head housekeeper had her "Immigration-fearing girls" clean the rooms without ever mentioning what they SO OBVIOUSLY knew about.

{Tatiana had her list of rooms and whether she was too tired to notice or the assignment sheet wasn't marked "properly" for "late check-out" or whatever, she stopped, unlocked the door without knocking first, and walked into Room 219. Several factors contributed to her not being able to make a quick exit; she was startled and scared that she'd lose her job when she realized there were people in the room, someone closed the door behind her, and she was quite stunned by the scene before her. [Note: It was quite literally a "scene". It was the filming of Scene 2 of "The Bellhop Bed Hop", written and directed by Giovanni Bodaccia and produced by VanDac Studios.]

Tatiana stood motionless, unable to tear her eyes away from the intense returning stares of the three young (about her age) and not exactly good-looking "actors/models"; a shaggy black-haired and very skinny, brown-skinned Hispanic guy wearing nothing, but sweat and a black vest, who was kneeling on the bed and thrusting into the upraised bottom of a completely naked, overly tanned, slightly overweight, and sun-bleached blonde white girl whose face's bottom half was buried and busy between the wide-open legs of what turned out to be her slightly less attractive and identical twin sister who was propped up on elbows with her back arched and head thrown back. It took Tatiana a moment to realize that she was being ushered toward the bed and, despite all of her "protesting", she made her film debut in that scene.}

Okay, I have to interject with some facts. Yes, Tatiana did appear in all eleven VanDac Studios' productions. However, just like in Scene 2 of "The Bellhop Bed Hop", she was never unclothed and never did she engage in the actual "act" with the actors/models. [Note: All models were eighteen or older at the time of filming and records are on file with a record keeper in Miami, Florida.] Actually, her appearances were nothing more than the camera filming from behind her as if you, me, what…(WHO)…ever were watching over her shoulder while she "observed".

Now, why do I know this? Alright, first, I can and will go to my grave honestly saying and knowing that I have ABSOLUTELY ZERO DESIRE to see any of my friends having sex, let alone seeing them naked, but I will admit that a couple of months ago after the many conversations with Tatiana that led her to tell me all about her life (everything prior to her coming to Obscurity was told to me by her and not by Lana or anyone else – I, honestly, don't think they know), I decided it was time to see her "films". So, you can think of me anyway you wish; a liar, a repressed horn-dog, a perv, or whatever else comes to your mind, but I really did it for research purposes. (Okay, second! I was curious, too! Sue me!) Anyway, I should tell you that they were not at all easy to find. [Note to Aggie: Don't know how you did it, but "Thanks".] Also, I don't think Tatiana knows that I've seen them.

{[Note: For whatever it's worth, VanDac Studios' name comes from Gio*VAN*ni Bo*DAC*cia.] After those first six uneventful months in Miami, the next six years did prove to be quite interesting for Tatiana. Two weeks after that fateful entrance into Room 219 she quit both of her jobs and married Gio (some footage of the small ceremony was spliced into "The Bellhop Bed Hop" right before the seven person finale orgy scene which includes the previously mentioned "bellhop", who appears in all five scenes, and three "bridesmaids" and three "groomsmen", none of whom were in or at Tatiana and Gio's actual ceremony). After that six months to get "The Bellhop Bed Hop" completed and released, the next three-and-a-half years and seven productions were spent around South Florida and Tatiana was "Set Designer" for VanDac Studios. During the next year's two productions, one filmed in New York City and the other around Southern California, Tatiana "wrote", while set designing, what would become VanDac Studios' final production, although, no one knew it at the time, which was filmed entirely in Italy. [Note: Tatiana based her "screenplay" in Italy because of Gio's roots and because she wanted to see Italy.]}

Okay, let me wrap this up in the quickest way possible to tell you how Tatiana came to Obscurity. She and Gio and their "stable" returned from Italy after three months. It was during the next few months that she realized her husband seemed quite preoccupied, less focused on and haphazard with his "editing", and just generally stressed and nervous. She tried to convince herself that he was trying too hard to make her film perfect, but in her heart of hearts she knew better. She wasn't stupid and she knew Gio was really just "small time". Also, she couldn't ignore the fact that "members" of The Viscinetti Family were making frequent visits, even though her husband tried to shield her from who they were by saying they were "interested parties" or something to that effect.

Now, I'm not going to lie. I did do a little research on The Viscinetti Family and they do (did?) seem to be as "viscious" and "Italian" as their name suggests. However, this is not about them and I'm not trying to get myself, Tatiana, or anyone else into any type of trouble, although, from what I can tell (the reason for the "did?"), they are no longer around or defunct, but, hey, let's use caution here. Anyway, suffice it to say, they seemed to have, and I honestly don't know a thing about mob stuff or want to, but they seemed to have "financed" VanDac Studios and weren't getting the return on their investment.

Finally, how Tatiana came to Obscurity! (I was trying to be quick, but it didn't quite work out that way…Oh well!) Remember the identical twin sisters from scene 2 of "The Bellhop Bed Hop"? Tatiana became friends, somewhat, with them during the filming and they talked about their upbringing in a small ideal town that they just had to "get the hell out of". They painted the picture so nice, even with their bad-mouthing of it, that Tatiana never forgot it and when Gio told her she needed to "go away" because she was in danger from The Viscinetti Family, she told him she'd go there (or come here, whatever) and wait for him. (I do not know why people tell me the things they do, but they do!) Anyway, I know and I know deep down that she knows that he'll never show up. (I mean, come on, it's been over twenty years, now, and you, I, and Tatiana knows he's dead! But, hey, who am I to squash a person's dreams?)

Okay, let me finish this up. What I heard from Lana about Tatiana the day after I arrived in Obscurity when she took me on the grand tour is, also, what intrigued me about her. All Lana could tell me about her is that she arrived some twenty years ago with two suitcases, the clothes on her back, and a wedding ring on her finger and she's always lived in the same low-rent apartment, worked at the same low-paying job, and (until me) has never really talked to anyone much more than to tell them she's married (NOT widowed). She was a woman of mystery!

Of course, everyone has been speculating that Tatiana and I are fooling around, although, no one has blatantly said it to my face, but they certainly do grill me in subtle and not-so-subtle ways to get me to spill the beans about her. I haven't. Oh, I don't think it is surprising that the only person who hasn't gotten upset with me for my "lack of gossip" is Lana.

Taking Walks

Two days into preparing to teach CW and PS during Teacher Preparation Week, I was prepared. There really wasn't much preparation to do because there were curriculum guidelines. Honestly? I think the week was for the teachers to get to know each other and form their own "clicks". It was kind of like being in a grown-up high school. Now, I'm not going to lie, I made some "friends", but with new friends come questions and I just wasn't ready to deal with all that. Luckily, I had the perfect excuse for getting out of being invited out after work and, even, to leave early the next few days.

Okay, again, before I continue, I have to say from personal past experience that I hate to lie because the lies will only come back to bite you on the ass. Now, this might not make a whole lot of sense at the moment because the whole pretext of my existence in Obscurity is a lie. Please bear with me, again. The big lies like my name, credentials, and such are easy to play off because they are constant. It's the little ones that can catch you up. Therefore, what I've found is that if you tell the truth in a general and vague sort of way people will jump to their own conclusions and if they ever come back and say that you said this, that, or the other, you can counter with what you actually said, the truth, and subtly let them know that they made up their own mind what that meant.

So, what was my excuse to get out of "social" interactions? I simply stated that I had just relocated and that I was still getting settled. And here's where my theory is substantiated. I had offers to help me move in, find a place to stay, stay with them until I could find a place because they had an empty guest room or whatever, paint, renovate, decorate, etcetera. Don't get me wrong, I TOTALLY APPRECIATE everyone's kindnesses, but, really, all I wanted to do was to be left alone. (Okay, wallow in my illness.) Anyway, I kindly refused every generous offer, thanked, and assured each person that if I needed anything at all that I'd be sure to call on them.

Where was I going with this? Oh yeah! I really WAS still trying to get settled so it wasn't an all out lie. My main focus at that point, however, was leaving Carlisle alone all day every day since I didn't have the luxury of being five minutes from home (like at Makker's bookstore) in case he didn't do his business in the morning before I headed off to work and I SO didn't want him doing his business on the floor of the apartment since he wasn't used to having a doggie door and because, whether or not he figured out that the doggie door was for him, there were only two reasons I could get him to leave the place without a leash; one was to go for a ride in the car and the other was to go down to Lana's. That's why I needed to get him into a "routine" as part of getting settled. [Note: It made sense. Maybe the long scenic route to sense, but it made it there nonetheless! Well, to me, anyway.]

Oh, some more background on Carlisle. He's totally a creature of habit. Not that we all aren't, but I think he is somewhat more than the rest of us. Anyway, it only took a couple of walks before he got his mind set on one particular route; right out of Lana's and down Heart Way, right on Lyons Road, right on Wellesley Lane, right on Kings Terrace, right back onto Heart Way to home all the while having to stop and sniff, pee, and poop in all the same places. And it was at his favorite pooping spot on Wellesley Lane that I met Ryan Fagan. [Note: Ryan has asked me on many occasions to call him by his nickname, Twinky, which was given to him by his "regular" group of friends in Whopping, but I just can't bring myself to and I still call him Ryan which is how he first introduced himself to me, but just so you know, I might refer to him as Twinky every now and again as it is pertinent.]

{Eighteen years ago, fifty-seven-year-old Patrick and fifty-year-old Maeve Fagan returned to Obscurity from Tokyo, Japan where they spent a year while Patrick was heading the legal team from *Levinson, Fagan, & Mancini* on behalf of the city of Whopping for the location of, construction of, and operation of an automobile factory (which was in existence for ten years before closing and putting hundreds and hundreds of Whopping, Obscurity, and nearby Gross County residents out of work) with their "unexpected surprise" of newborn baby boy Seamus (pronounced "SHAY-mus") Ryan Fagan.

The Fagan's baby was probably MORE unexpected and MORE surprising to those who knew Patrick and Maeve (and even those who didn't know them because rumors circulated) for several reasons. The first obviously being Maeve's age. Then there was the fact that when they left for

Tokyo, the youngest of their four sons had just graduated high school and ever since he was born eighteen years earlier Maeve had adamantly stated that she was done having children. There was, also, the fact that, except for the occasional business social engagement in the previous several years, Patrick and Maeve were never seen together and, of course, the rumor mill of Patrick's affair with his administrative assistant Donna Distrada (who didn't return from Tokyo – and if she did, it was elsewhere). Finally, the newborn infant seemed "a little big" for being a newborn.}

Okay, I just want to make clear that I've never met Ryan's father, Patrick, who's been dead for seven years, or his mother, Maeve, who has spent the last year, since Ryan graduated high school, "traveling" between Chicago and Scottsdale (depending on time of year weather) and "staying" with two of the first four boys, second oldest Michael and youngest Conor, and their families, so I can only speculate and report the rumors as I've heard them from Lana, others I've met in Obscurity, and from Ryan himself who's sworn me to secrecy about everything he's told me about himself so he can continue to receive his "monthly allowance" from his brother the attorney, Michael, in Chicago, so as not to, as Michael says, "Shame us," which is how he's able to maintain, at the (now) age of nineteen and without working, a "household" on his own in The Heights. [Note: I've REALLY tried to be as concise and as UNconfusing as possible and, after several attempts, I hope that I've succeeded.]

So, I guess the next thing to tell you is how Ryan got his nickname. Let me start by saying that Ryan is gay. I wasn't surprised when he finally told me and I had pretty much figured it out when I first saw him. Also, I think at first he had a "crush" on me. Okay, I know he did because I found (and I say "found" because they were left out in an obvious place) some doodlings of his name, Ryan, with mine, Autumns, and different ways of interconnecting his name, Ryan, with my name, Ryder. [Note: The boy is a very talented artist!] Anyway, if I was gay and into young men I have to say that I'd be VERY LUCKY to have him and probably would be VERY JEALOUS.

Now, in a way I am jealous! Not of anyone interested in Ryan and I do hope that he finds the man of his dreams some day, but of his youthful beauty. Before I continue, I'm thrilled to be my age and I don't think I make small children run away screaming in fear at the sight of me, however, I was never as good looking as him. [Note: I am completely heterosexual AND I am secure enough to find and comment on beauty in BOTH sexes and the boy IS beautiful and I'm jealous because I don't think

I ever was!] I hope he doesn't get angry with me with the description I'm about to write of him. I hope he sees it and maybe uses it to his advantage if he ever decides to place a "personal ad" on some internet singles' site.

Ryan is about five-feet-nine/ten-inches tall, an inch or so taller than me. He is lanky, maybe around a-hundred-and-fifty-five pounds, but with a natural, un-athletic athletic build. His youthfully smooth and lightly hairy skin is slightly darker than the pale skin of his Irish parents and slightly lighter than that of, I'm assuming by her name that she's of Italian descent, Donna Distrada. He, also, like Donna (I've seen the picture he has of her for some reason), has thick, black wavy hair, his is longish and unkempt, as opposed to the coarse reddish-brown of his parents and siblings, eyes the color of coal, not a hazely-brown, and kind of a long and angular-ish face, unlike the round and ruddy of his family. [Note: I'm not jumping to any conclusions here!]

So, NOW, you're thinking I'm some closeted "troll" (an older gay man after young guys – I know the lingo – two of my very good friends ARE lesbians and I AM a writer) because of the picture I've painted of Ryan and because of the MORE general and LESS descriptive pictures I've painted of Lana and Tatiana. You're wrong, but you are entitled to your opinion! Anyway, the two main reasons for this are that I know neither Lana nor Tatiana are looking for anyone and I really like Ryan and I really want him to find the man who truly loves him (not just for his looks, but, hey, you gotta start somewhere and it's really not a bad place to start) for him. [Note to…I'm not sure who: I do fear that if Ryan reads this, although, I do hope he does for other reasons, he'll move back to his crush thinking that there may possibly be a chance of a romantic life together. There isn't.]

Okay, like I started, let me move on to how Ryan got his nickname, Twinky. In "gay terminology", a "Twink" is a young, of age (I hope! And I'm going with that!) to EARLY twenties gay boy…young man…BOY (?!?). Ryan is nineteen and prefers older men (hence ME, I guess) and his regular group of friends in Whopping, as I mentioned previously, are older (anywhere from thirty-five on) gay men who I've met as I've accompanied Ryan on a few occasions (I'm open to new experiences both as a writer and a person because it can only help me to grow in both respects) to parties, dinner or otherwise, and it's his chosen group of older friends who gave him his nickname.

So, I didn't use Ryan's nickname from my perspective after all. I didn't think I would, but I like to leave things open just in case. Anyway, as much as I feel that Ryan had a crush on me, I DO THINK that his initial interest in me was by way of Carlisle (Am I jealous? Who knows!?!) and by the way he (Ryan) ran up to "us" on one of those first routine walks. One thing I do know is I felt I was slowly moving down the list of Carlisle's favorite people. Especially when I started letting him stay with Ryan while I was at work.

Starting School

It didn't take but a few days for both Carlisle and me (I hate to admit that I'm probably just as much of a creature of habit as he is) to fall into our routine. Luckily, both of my morning classes didn't start until nine o'clock, however, I still had to be up by six to jump in the shower and then throw something on to take Carlisle out to take a "frantic" pee (that usually takes about ten minutes), then shave (I prefer to shave after I've showered because I'm more awake and my skin is dryer after washing than having the daily and overnight oily build-up), then the slow trek halfway around the block to Ryan's to drop off Carlisle (I honestly thought Ryan was pulling my leg when he offered, I mean, him being young and single and on his own and all, but he was up and waiting each morning) and have a cup of coffee, then back around the block to dress and finish getting ready for work, and then off, on most mornings, to The Obscurity Eatery for breakfast (some mornings I ate with Lana), then the thirty-five minute drive to Whopping. After the afternoon classes were over, I'd drive straight to Ryan's to pick up Carlisle (and sit and talk or eat with Ryan if he'd "just prepared" something, but "made too much") and this way Carlisle thought he was getting a car ride every day then home and sometimes have dinner with Lana. [Note: Dinners with Tatiana didn't start happening until after Thanksgiving.]

So, my anal retentiveness aside, I, also, crave a routine so I don't have to think. It's not that I'm a scatterbrain or flighty or anything, I just need structure. Now, I'm not to the point where my closet is filled with the same shirt, tie, pants, and jacket times seven, but I will admit that I do pick out what I'm going to wear the next day the night before. See, its life's little decisions that tend to bog me down and rattle my nerves and (I hope this doesn't sound awful) it's one of the things I miss most about Lois. She understood my "quirky" nature and pretty much kept me grounded. Okay, this might seem like a really big stretch to where I'm headed, but it's this

27

need for structure and routine that allowed me to justify (at the time and in my head) using one of my colleagues, Constance Mattering the Culinary Arts and Restaurant and Catering Management teacher.

Constance was a "JonBenet" before anyone knew who JonBenet Ramsey was and could make that reference. And, of course, Constance is still, well, very much…Constance. [Note: Did you think I was going to say, "Alive?"] Anyway, young Constance, not Connie or anything else, was obviously a child beauty queen. She won her first title, Miss Cicada, the four to nine-year-old version, anyway (there was, IS, a pre-teen, teen, and regular - ??? - version, also), in Gross County which, as I mentioned previously, is on the opposite side of Whopping than Obscurity. Actually, it is her only title because she never entered another beauty pageant after winning and she reigned for seventeen years because all age group versions of the Miss Cicada Beauty Pageants only happen during the Gross County Cicada Festival every seventeen years when the ugly little buggers (the cicadas that is) are out in full force. Her reign ended four years ago when she was twenty-six and that's when she moved to Whopping and started teaching at the community college.

Alrighty! I know you know that I moved away from my, as you've come to expect, "flashback" of Constance's life, but this is really the most interesting part of it and I honestly don't know how else to tell it. Also, and I've never thought about it before, but I guess why I never got all of the "dish" on her and her family is because nobody in Obscurity, but me, has ever met her or her family. And I've never invited her to my place or to any functions here because I didn't want to give her the wrong impression. I have been asked on several occasions by Lana, though, to do so. Anyway, it's not that the rest of her life is UNinteresting, but it's pretty normal.

She was born, grew up, and graduated high school with a B average in Green Haven. She didn't have some controlling "stage" mother and disinterested, or otherwise, father. It was her idea to start doing pageants, much to her parents' chagrin, although they supported her, when she was six and saw her first televised beauty pageant. She attended Shrewesburg University for six years where she got her Master's in Culinary Arts. After she got her Master's, Cornelia Stokes, the owner of Cornelia's Place where Constance worked while attending college, made her the restaurant manager which is what she did for the next two years until she crowned the now eleven-year-old and current Miss Cicada of the four to nine-year-old version of the pageant. She then came to Whopping and has taught Culinary Arts and Restaurant and Catering Management and seems perfectly happy. Except for being unmarried, not that she's depressed or suicidal about that.

Oh, one theory I have about her "marital" status is her looks. To the average guy, and let's be honest, most men, despite some of their machismo attitudes, are average, so her looks can be rather intimidating. She's five-foot-seven and looks like a Barbie doll. She has straight blonde hair just past her shoulders, but cut to perfectly frame her tanned, long, and oval face, emerald green eyes that COMMAND your attention, but don't DEMAND it, and a perfectly rounded, yet ski-sloped nose just the right distance above her not too thin and too pouty lips. Her long thin neck leading down to her...Okay, I'm back. WHEW!!! Wish I still smoked. JUST KIDDING! But you get the idea. Beauty AND brains.

Now, I do have another quick theory as well. The woman NEVER shuts up! Her constant smattering and incessant babbling can be VERY trying and annoying. I'm assuming that it stems from those few years early on of beauty pageant "interviews", although, I don't know. I said it was just a theory. Anyway, this is another reason for me not going into the whole life of Constance Alayna Mattering; she would go off into so many tangents while babbling that I usually tuned her out.

Okay, I have to tell you how I "used" her. As I said earlier, I found Obscurity while searching for some place to base my new novel in and the few hours I had in between my morning and afternoon classes turned out to be very productive for it. For the first couple of days, anyway. Then I started getting visits from Constance and I pretended right along with her, not that she totally pretended, that she was just sharing the wealth of food from her class's daily "projects" and wasn't trying to find her way to a man's heart through his stomach. Okay, maybe I AM an asshole, but I was a hungry asshole and it kept me from having to "decide" where to run out and get a bite to eat every day or, more importantly, having to throw something together and take a lunch.

In my defense, she really wasn't all that annoying and I was, okay, AM, attracted to her and I probably could have used her for Camarada, Leslie, and Makker's cure for my illness, but this is another reason for my defense that I'm not an asshole. I believe that there are only two reasons to ask someone out on a date; one is if you are trying to get in a relationship and the other is to "get some". I believe that if you are going to engage in sexual activity you should be in a relationship. I'm not looking for a relationship. Ergo, well, you can do the math. Also, she's ten years younger than me and

I just cannot be one of those men! So, I was using, but, at the same time, WASN'T using Constance.

Doing Chores

I'd been in Obscurity for a week-and-a-half when I "met" Eddie Ottsovont or Eddie-Os as he's called now and I will explain why in a moment. Anyway, it was Saturday after my first week of school and I guess I was still invigorated from my new surroundings and job and I woke up around seven without the alarm on and took Carlisle out for a leisurely pee and realized that the grass was looking a bit long and unkempt. Now, I know I pay rent to Lana and am not expected to do any of the upkeep chores around the place, but I felt a familial obligation nonetheless. Also, I WANTED to do it. God only knows why. At forty-three I'd never mowed a lawn in my life. Anyway, after I took Carlisle back up to the apartment and threw on something to get dirty in, I went back down and started rooting through the shed at the back of the yard not too far from the stairs. Luckily, it wasn't locked and there was a lawnmower in it.

Okay, so, how was I forty-three without ever mowing a lawn? Let me backtrack for you for a sec. Lois and I bought a condo which is technically still my home address and there are groundskeepers. Apartment living from the time I moved out on my own until Lois and I bought the condo, so, other groundskeepers. Growing up and living with my parents, I have a brother one year older than me and it was his weekly chore to mow the lawn. Mine was to clean the swimming pool. Not a bad gig for two bucks a week! Well, that's what it started at, but it did go up slightly over the years.

So, I had the lawnmower out and I was just pulling and pulling on that stupid starter cord and it wasn't doing a goddamn thing for me. Sorry, it still pisses me off. Anyway, after a few minutes, to no avail, and being somewhat exhausted, I decided to sit and rest a minute and go over in my head what my brother used to do and what I'd seen others throughout my life do. I couldn't come up with ANYTHING I was doing wrong or different. So, with a surge of adrenaline and the determination that I was going to get that freakin' thing going, I got up, literally spit on my hands and rubbed them together, and leaned down to pull that sonofabitch to life. It's when I started to lean down that I heard a scream and was tackled to the ground.

Now, I'm not what anyone would consider a big or strong guy, but, hey, I'm not little AND I am scrappy. I'm five-foot-eight, a-hundred-and-forty-ish pounds, and I have only eleven percent body fat. Not that that makes a whole lot of difference when you're underneath a seven-thousand pound linebacker. Okay, I'm over-exaggerating at the moment, but in the midst of my fright and panic that's what it seemed like. Oh, and the one thing that still gets my goat, even though I know better now, is how Lana came up and pulled that six foot, two-hundred-and-seventy pound, brown-haired, and bearded hulk off of me with only her fingers on his shirt collar. So much for being "not little" and "scrappy"!

I know. You want to know if that's what actually happened. Actually it is. [Note: Somehow in the midst of all the "turmoil" I was not only a participant, but an observer, too. I'll chalk that up to being the "A+ student in Observation" that I mentioned previously.] However, what I learned after we had a moment to "cool off in our corners" was that Eddie came to Lana's every other Saturday to mow her yard with "his" lawnmower and being the, and I don't know how else to say this because I'm not trying to be mean or degrading, "simple-minded" man that he is, he just got a surge of anger and was protecting her and the lawnmower.

Oh, I must, also, say that as simple-minded that he is, he is very intelligent in a lot of intriguing ways, too. And that's where in some circles of society he would be called an "idiot savant" and that's why I used simple-minded so as not to be mean or degrading. Plus, I really like Eddie-Os. Anyway, to make a long story short, if I'm not too late, Lana introduced us formally after we both cooled off and I realized who he was from when Lana pointed him out at the festival the previous Saturday and everything she told me about him during the grand tour came flooding back into my mind.

{The Ottsovont clan, of which there aren't as many now as there was over two hundred years ago, didn't found Obscurity, but was found just shortly after Obscurity was established in the EXTREMELY early 1800's. They have always been a very "close-knit" family. So much so that only every now and again does someone unrelated get brought into the family to introduce new DNA into it. Eddie at thirty-three is one of the last of the generation conceived before new breeding stock was somehow convinced to join the clan. [Note: Lana has on a few occasions "explained" Eddie's lineage, but I do get really confused with the whole father/brother/cousin marrying the sister/daughter/niece "family tree" so I'm not even going to attempt explaining it to you, not that I could.]}

Okay, I'm just as guilty as the next person for in my life making jokes or teasing remarks about someone being "inbred". Also, I can, just like the next person, pretty much tell when there's a resemblance among family members. The funny thing is (and I don't mean "funny ha-ha" and I'm not trying to be...oh, what's a good word? Condescending? Not really, but, anyway) that until I met Eddie and some of his family, I didn't put the two together and that you CAN actually tell if there is inbreeding going on because, well, there is this "family resemblance" that FAR surpasses normal (???) family resemblance. [Note: It's really kind of, I don't know how else to say it, but to say, "Oogie."]

Anyway, let me just move on. The reason I and everyone else now calls him Eddie-Os is because when we finished doing the lawn work together that first Saturday, for some reason when he was leaving I said, "Adios!" He started laughing and jumping up and down and started yelling, "Eddie-Os!" over and over. It's just sorta stuck. So, now I guess I should tell you how Eddie came to be Lana's "groundskeeper".

{The Ottsovont clan's land is a couple miles into the woods behind The Deladees' first home and business. When Eddie was old enough to start venturing away on his own, he kept showing up at the garage. He was never in the way, but his presence was known. Lana tried on many occasions to take the dirty, ratty-clothed, and emaciated boy food and clothes outgrown or unwanted by her boys only to scare the boy running off quickly into the woods. Eventually she started leaving those things out in the back before he'd arrive. Much to her delight, the food was always eaten and the clothes would be gone.

It was after a couple of years of this when Lana finally decided to ready herself and lay in wait for the boy. She put a plate of leftovers from the previous night's dinner in the same spot, an old car door placed on top of some crates like a table, as she always did and hid in the bushes. She just stayed there watching and waiting for a couple of hours after he'd eaten until he was bored with his tinkering around and followed him into the woods. When she came upon the clearing of the ramshackle Ottsovont cabin, she remained hidden until a woman, she assumed it was the boy's mother (and she was right), emerged to do some outdoor chores.

Lana was a little taken aback by Bertie Ottsovont's outrage over finding out what Eddie had been doing, even though Lana assured her that it was perfectly fine, and even more taken aback by Bertie's outrage at her for her "charity" that they didn't need. The next day when she took out a plate of food, much to her dismay she found all of the clothes she'd left for Eddie over the past couple of years still neatly folded, clearly unworn, and piled on top of the makeshift table. Also, to her dismay she didn't see Eddie for three months, even though she continued to take a plate of food to the table every day.

As nice and easy going as Lana is, she's, also, very headstrong. That afternoon at the end of three months, she went through every closet and drawer in the house, much to her children's dismay (and that's putting it lightly), collected everything that she'd not seen them, her husband, or herself wear regularly, completely bared the kitchen cupboards, loaded down her family with bags and bags…and bags, and marched them off into the woods as the sun was starting to set to The Ottsovont's cabin.}

Suffice it to say there was a lot of yelling and cussing (gunshots have never been confirmed), but The Deladees returned home late that night empty handed. Also, Eddie began doing odd jobs around the house and garage for Lana and "fair wages" the next day. When Larry retired and they moved to The Heights, Eddied started showing up on their front porch each morning at eight o'clock. Lana didn't have the heart to turn him away, especially after he'd walked so far, so she made a deal with him to come by every other Saturday and she would have a list of things for him to do. He declined the offer of her or Larry going to pick him up.

Hey, tidbit of info, if you've never started a lawnmower and are going to try it, you have to push this little rubbery button three times and then pull and hold the thin handly bar thingy up to the handle you hold onto while mowing while you pull the starter cord. Eddie taught me all that. Of course, he used all the technical names which I can't seem to remember. Oh yeah, except for a few times which I can count on one hand, I'm up and ready to assist Eddie with the yard work every other Saturday. And once in a while he lets me run the mower! Especially if Carlisle wants to come down and play with him. Oh yes, I realized I was down another place on the list of Carlisle's favorite people.

Shaping Up

Breakfasts…and lunches…and dinners…oh my!
Breakfasts and lunches and dinners, oh my!
BREAKFASTS AND LUNCHES AND DINNERS, OH MY!
BREAKFASTSANDLUNCHESANDDINNERSOHMY!

Let me start with the obvious. I got fat! Yes, I topped out at one-hundred-and-fifty-six pounds! Okay, to most that might not seem fat, but when you've weighed one-thirty-five to one-forty since you were fourteen its fat. Besides, the men in my family don't start getting guts until around their mid-fifties. So, I still had (have) a good ten to fifteen years to go! Anyway, it took a couple of months, but it happened. I don't know why it surprised me, I mean, daily breakfasts with Lana, Ryan, and/or at The Obscurity Eatery, Constance's huge lunch spreads, and then dinner with Ryan and/or Lana. Duh! [Note: The "Duh" is for me.] Oh, and to top it off…the holidays were fast approaching. More food! Aaahhhh!

Yes, the holidays were fast approaching. Once Halloween is over its pretty much bing (Thanksgiving), bang (Christmas), boom (New Year's) without really much time to think between one and the next. Before I continue, I guess I should, for posterity's sake, anyway, mention that I went to a very interesting Halloween party at Ryan's invitation at Ruby's Slippers; one of Whopping's two gay clubs. When Ryan invited me, I made a joke that he should go as "Twinkie The Kid". I thought, of course, after I said it that I'd have to go into the whole long explanation of who that snack food cartoon character from my childhood was, but I didn't. Why? Because Ryan immediately said that I could go as "Captain Cupcake" and he would take care of putting together our costumes. All I'm going to say about his versions of the two characters is that they were gayer, more adult, and had a very creative way of denoting the cream filling. [Note: As I said, he's very artistic. Also, it was a blast! The party, that is.]

Okay, back to my weight problem and how I decided to solve it. I did think about longer walks with Carlisle and walking around campus in between my classes. The former never happened and the latter lasted all of one walk. And a very short one at that. It was during that one very short walk that I recollected the gym just down the street from the college that I passed on my way to and from home each day. Now, I know walking seems a lot easier, but I do kind of lack self discipline. Anyway, I thought it couldn't hurt to at least check it out.

One week later I did. I had sat for fifteen minutes in practically non-moving traffic behind a three car fender bender when I decided to scooch over into the middle turn lane and pull into a shopping center's parking lot to turn around and attempt another way home. It happened to be the shopping center that the gym was in and I decided that it was a sign from above.

Now, it's probably not hard to believe that I'd never worked out a day in my life. Well, other than the normal every day lifting of things and whatnot that we do and convince ourselves that we are physically active people. I can personally attest that those things we do in no way, shape, or form even begin to pass for working out. I found that out after I signed up for a year, ran into the athletic apparel store at the other end of the shopping center (I know, why not next door?) and dropped, CHARGED, slightly over two-hundred dollars on workout clothes, sneakers, a bag for all my gear, and a padlock for a locker, went back to the gym, changed into one of my color coordinated outfits that the very nice salesgirl had helped me pick out, and went out to the free weight area and picked up two twenty-five pound dumbbells...and immediately set them back down.

About ten minutes later, I'm sure eight of which it took me to finally admit defeat and pick up two five-pound dumbbells and the other two to awkwardly find a very secluded spot far away from and out of sight of the other people there, a guy who was younger and really not much bigger than me, but definitely toned and in shape, came over and casually mentioned that the gym did have personal trainers for a nominal fee, at least to help one get started. I thanked him and said it was my first time there and I was just checking the place out. I then pretended to lift the five-pound weights for a few minutes, then walked around for a while and pretended to check out some of the machines, then went to the locker room and stuffed my regular clothes into my bag and just got the hell out of there.

A week later, after Ryan and Lana's continual prodding, I returned and asked, while signing in, to meet with a personal trainer. Oh yeah, that's when I started wearing just some cotton shorts and t-shirts that I wear around the house. The reason being, when I finally showed up to pick up Carlisle from Ryan's the previous week in my workout outfit because I just had to "get the hell out of the gym", Ryan was nice enough to hoot and holler, but it wasn't easy for him in between his outbursts of laughter. Lana pretty much had the same reaction when I got home a few minutes later. I'm sure, also, if Carlisle could have, he would have!

Anyway, another reason why it took a week to go back is, and I was really more surprised by Lana than Ryan, the way each of them kept going on about "the hot, young muscle gods/studs/jocks" that would be there. Of course, Lana didn't quite go there like Ryan did, but she did nonetheless… Hhhhmmmmm. So, it was the thought of being ridiculed and laughed at by a bunch of "muscle head jocks" that kept me from going back immediately. Okay, it was the thought of the thirty-five dollar monthly fee charged to my credit card for the next year, whether or not I went, that finally convinced me to return…and ask for a personal trainer…for a nominal additional fee…and repeat over and over AND OVER in my mind that the muscle head jock was just to get me started.

I'd been waiting for about five minutes by the check-in desk after I'd changed clothes (and I'd just about convinced myself to leave and never return) when the guy who came up and told me about personal trainers at the gym the week before came up and introduced himself as my personal trainer (needless to say I was VERY relieved) and we sat and talked for about twenty minutes about what it was that I wanted to accomplish so he could put together a personal regimen for me. My main goal obviously was to lose the inner tube that had become attached to my midsection to which he told me that lifting weights was totally the wrong thing to do which led me to confessing the whole five-pound dumbbell fiasco and that maybe it wouldn't hurt to build up a little strength in the process. He was kind enough to pretend not to remember that.

So, after a month of my three day a week workout routine, I noticed the inner tube was deflating and I actually started moving up in weight (lifting) and resistance, but it made it easier for me to have someone motivate me so I didn't give up. Also, it really was a nominal fee. Plus, I liked the guy and we had a lot in common. Okay, maybe not a WHOLE lot, but he is a widower, too. [Note: I felt it pointless to go into the whole thing about Lois and I not being legally married, etcetera. I just referred to her as my wife.]

{Robert James "Jim" Traynor and Candice Marjorie "Candi" Majewski met at Shrewesburg University during their freshman year while working towards Bachelor's Degrees in Health and Physical Education. Jim was born and raised in Gross Springs and went to Shrewe U the year after he graduated high school. Candi, on the other hand, took a year off after graduating Whopping Senior High School and backpacked through Europe before attending the university. It was love at first sight for both of them. The moment they saw each other and locked eyes they knew they were destined to be together, however, they waited until the summer after freshman year to tie the knot.

Upon graduating with their degrees, they found that Jim's high school alma mater in Gross Springs had openings for both "men's" and "women's" Physical Education teachers. They applied and were accepted. For the eight years they taught there they were adored by the students and faculty alike. They were even voted "Hottest Teacher Couple" for the yearbook all eight years. And why wouldn't they be? Mrs. Majewski-Traynor was five-eight, with short strawberry-blonde hair, but long enough to "scrunch" into a pony-tail, and had the body of a beach volleyball Olympian. Mr. Traynor, also at five-eight, with buzzed dishwater-blonde hair, and a swimmer's build, made the perfect match for his wife.

Candi didn't want her husband to associate his birthday with the day he found out his wife had cancer, especially not his thirtieth birthday and to be presented with the gift that she had Ovarian Cancer. However, even with the extravagant surprise party she'd put together and all of the diversions, he knew something was wrong. She had to tell him that she just found out from her doctor that day. They moved to Whopping from Gross Springs three years later (two years ago) to be near her family when the cancer returned. Candice Marjorie Majewski-Traynor died six months later at the age of thirty-four.}

I guess I should tell you what other things Jim Traynor and I have in common besides both being widowers. Even though he is eight years younger than me and seems to be dealing with the loss of his soul mate a whole lot better than me, which makes neither of us less of a man because we all deal with our grief in our own ways, Lois was older than me, too, but by three years, not one, and she, too, died from Ovarian Cancer. [Note: Just thought you should know.]

Okay, I'm going to wrap this up with some very good advice that Jim gave me that first day that he introduced the gym to me and it has stuck with me and I've tried to and somewhat succeeded with incorporating it into other aspects of my life. He said, "Leave your self-consciousness at the door. Everyone had to start." He was, IS, right. I leave my self-consciousness at the entrance to the gym every time I walk in. I, also, try very hard to leave it at the entrance of every "other place" that I enter.

Helping Out

Camarada, Leslie, and Makker were hounding me (and Carlisle) to return home for Thanksgiving. And as much as I wanted to I just couldn't. Not because of lack of time off, it was Thanksgiving Break (not that they knew that), but because I knew they would join forces and riddle me with rapid fire (albeit "friendly fire") questions of where I'd been and what I'd been up to. I just wasn't ready to deal with all that. Of course, there were subtle and not-so-subtle guilt trips, but I held firm my ground.

Now, I will say that the worst guilt trip came from Makker, although, I don't really think he meant it that way. See, shortly after I left he attended an African Literary Conference at the university to learn of African literature he might not have been aware of so as to extend his "Cultural" section of his bookstore. What he didn't expect was to be attracted to one of the guest speakers; one Professor Innig Geliefde visiting from the Institute of African Studies in Ibadan, Nigeria.

Long story short, the conference he attended was the last of a year long U.S. tour and after spending the evening together talking after the conference and being absolutely inseparable for the remaining week, she was able to extend her Visa by accepting a teaching position at the university there. So, where does the guilt trip come in? Makker wanted me to meet her before and be there when he "popped the question" on Thanksgiving. I really wanted to meet Innig and be there for my friend, but I still held firm my ground.

Oh, so, what DID I do for Thanksgiving? Well, that's not exactly a great segue, but sometimes, and I'm pretty sure you've come to realize this about me by now, I just have to go where my mind takes me so I'll just go on. I accepted an invitation I never even thought of.

Since I frequented The Obscurity Eatery, I guess it's not surprising that I came to know, sort of, anyway, the owner/proprietor Kurtwood Lewis Mudgeon, II. Now, not everyone in Obscurity is "peachy-keen and jelly beans" and Kurt Mudgeon is the attestment to that. He is EXACTLY what Lana refers to him as, lovingly and with respect, of course, "That curmudgeonly old bastard!" [Note: It makes me laugh because Lana doesn't EVER use curse words.] Anyway, I, of course, have adopted the "term of endearment".

Okay, before I go on, I should remind you of Obscurity's racial make-up. Out of one-thousand-seven-hundred-and-fifty-five Obscurity residents, one-thousand-seven-hundred-and-twenty are White, twenty-six are Hispanic/Latino, and the nine remaining are African American, Asian, Native American, Other, or Bi-racial. Kurt Mudgeon is one of "the nine remaining". He is the one and only African American that I've encountered in Obscurity. [Note: To be clear, I do mean JUST Obscurity not Whopping.]

Now, that curmudgeonly old bastard was born and has lived his whole life in Obscurity, so obviously he wasn't always the only African American resident. As of the year 2010 census he is, but previous censuses (Is that the correct plural form?) included a larger number of African American residents. [Note: You are probably not surprised, as I wasn't, by this information. Oh! I'm not going into a whole history of African Americans in Obscurity.]

Okay, I've got to let you know something else before I go on. I'm not really as politically correct as I guess I've tried to make myself sound. Don't get me wrong, I'm all for POLITICAL CORRECTNESS in the correct arena, but I just have to say that I prefer the term, "Black." Why? Well, in my younger years I worked very closely with a dark-skinned girl (young woman, my age) and in conversation one day she told me how other people referred to her as African American (she never corrected them), but she was Spanish American. Also, there's the whole news report/reporter thing when they say, "An African American and a White." Anyway, and you can think of me however you want, again, BUT if I'm expected to make a correct lineage reference by the way a person looks then I should be correctly identified as an English French Dutch German American upon sight. Not trying to get preachy, just trying to explain myself.

So, down off my "soapbox" I will tell you that I am curious about Kurt's life and why he is so "curt" and "brusque". Honestly? I don't know! What I have come to realize is that sometimes you just have to accept people for the way they are and move on. And I guess it's his curtness and brusqueness that has kept me from learning so much about him and why I've never really been able to get any "real" info on him from anyone. Lana especially. I do have to say, however, I'm not really that surprised that I never got a lot of info on him from Tatiana seeing how she's got her own stuff going on.

Okay, what I can tell you about Kurt, besides him being six-feet tall (if he could stand up straight – I assume it's from the many years of bending over as he prepared meals), skinny as a rail, completely bald, and with a snow white moustache that stands out against his muddy coffee complexion but is somehow still obscured by his wide nostril-prominent nose, is that he's seventy-eight-years old, he inherited The Obscurity Eatery from his father, Kurtwood Lewis (I), and his mother, Anna Mary, and he is the youngest and only son of the eleven children born to his parents.

What I can also tell you is that a couple of his sisters are still living and there are a lot of nieces and nephews (seconds, thirds, and fourths) scattered around the country, but he was never married, so, I really don't know if the Mudgeon name will carry on. [Note: I probably could have made him more colorful, no pun intended, but it probably would have bored you to tears as much as it did me.]

So, where was I going with this? Don't you just love a "train of thought derailment"? Give me a sec. Camarada, Leslie, and Makker…Guilt trips… Professor Innig Geliefde…Popping the question…Thanksgiving…The Obscurity Eatery…OH YEAH! THE INVITATION! Duh! Okay, back on track.

Since I frequented The Obscurity Eatery, I guess it's not surprising that Kurt Mudgeon came to know me somewhat, too. And it's because he knew of my "just visiting" status that he knew I didn't have family here and pretty much figured that I'd be free to help out with his annual, and this is where he DOES become peachy-keen and jelly beans and why he's called "that curmudgeonly old bastard" WITH LOVE AND RESPECT, Thanksgiving feast donation of food and time preparing and serving at a homeless shelter in Whopping. I, of course, agreed. And I would have anyway even without him putting Tatiana up to help coerce me. Now, I will admit that I took it a step further. Before even asking Lana and Ryan to volunteer their time, I volunteered their time. Luckily, both were eager to accept MY invitation. Thank goodness!

Oh, as I said earlier, it was after this that my dinners with Tatiana began. Actually they weren't always just the two of us, although the majority of them were, but sometimes Ryan and/or Lana would go or one of them would host the rest of us. Kurt never accepted our constant invitations. [Note: This is honestly JUST BECAUSE, but if Kurt Mudgeon has a "term of endearment" for me I don't know what it is AND honestly it's really neither here nor there. Okay, I don't REALLY want to know what it is either if he does.]

Spreading Cheer

I STILL don't know how the hell it happened, but it did! Okay, I do, but still. Anyway, I guess the best way to start this is to ask a question. (A rhetorical question obviously.) Have you ever been so caught up in the moment of one thing that you agree to another? Even if YOU haven't, I have. And that's how I got "roped into" accepting being in charge of the faculty Christmas party.

As I look back on this my mind still reels and I can only say, and PLEASE pardon my French, but, "What the fuck was I thinking?!?" Yes, I do know what was going through my head. I was so wrapped up in the excitement of doing something "charitable and selfless" with the whole Thanksgiving thing that when Constance nominated me and there were "seconds" on the nomination (I now realize it was because no one else wanted the headaches), I felt jazzed enough to accept. I did return the favor to Constance, however. She was, IS, the Culinary Arts and the Restaurant and Catering Management teacher and I roped her into helping. Actually I really should have thought of this when I did my roping of her, but she was all too eager to help because it meant more time with me.

Oh! It did give her the perfect Final Exams for her classes, too. Her Culinary Arts students planned the menu and prepared the food for the party and her Restaurant and Catering Management students planned the party from finding a location permitted for a cash bar to designing, decorating, seating, and serving. [Note: I don't know what the individual students got as grades, but the entire affair was an A++ in my book. Okay, it helped that all I really had to do was approve/veto EVERY FINE LITTLE DETAIL that they came up with.]

Now, in addition to overseeing Constance's students' plans I did have to find musical entertainment. Ryan suggested an "up'n'coming (all Caucasian, all virgin, all gay) boy band" called The Tighty Whiteys that was emerging on the scene in the gay clubs around Whopping and Gross County, but I opted for a DJ instead. I also had to find a Santa and Mrs. Claus; it was after all a Christmas party. I did let Ryan be a part, somewhat, of the planning, though. I agreed to let him be an elf since I didn't take him up on his offer of getting the band. And I let him design his elf costume himself. [Note: It was tasteful (I wasn't too worried) and it did garner him a brief affair with one of my colleagues; the Accounting II teacher BN Thayer Dunnthatt. Everyone calls him Ben, like that actor from *Too Close for Comfort*, JM "Jim" J Bullock.]

Alright, I have to say that I do have a "certain skepticism" when it comes to relationships. This doesn't stem from my relationship with Lois, but I have learned in my years that AFFAIRS OF THE HEART can only be learned, never taught. I only mention this because after I learned from Ryan that he and Ben were starting to see each other I fought myself over and over about telling Ryan that I'd overheard Ben on a few occasions telling another gay male teacher, as they were eyeing some of the male student bodies, that he'd "been there, done that". Needless to say I never did mention this to Ryan. [Note: Ryan didn't seem particularly hurt when the affair ended.]

{Beatrice Margaret "Betty" Thayer married Eugene Newton "Newtie" Dunnthatt when she found out she was pregnant. [Notes: She wasn't pregnant by him and nobody but Betty knows who the actual father is, but she did rush over and sleep with Newtie the next day after finding out she was pregnant. Newtie found this out later. And I found everything out from Ryan as he found it out from Ben.] Even though the Thayer-Dunnthatt engagement announcement and wedding was "rushed" so Betty wasn't showing and could still wear white, it was to go down in Whopping history as one of the most elaborate social events.

Whopping's publishing magnate of The Whopping Post, John Peter Thayer (he inherited the newspaper from his father-in-law), stopped the presses of that Sunday's edition to add the Thayer-Dunnthatt engagement announcement when his wife Beverly Diane, along with their "teary-eyed" seventeen-year-old daughter and their daughter's "very nervous" nineteen-year-old boyfriend, informed him of Betty's "current situation" that Saturday night. In addition to the engagement announcement it was announced that the "happy occasion" would be held on Beatrice Margaret's eighteenth birthday two weeks away because the couple was "so much in love".

Frederick Eugene and Elizabeth Gertrude Dunnthatt, owners and operators of the three Palace Jewelers in Whopping, were thrilled that their son Newtie was marrying into the Thayer "dynasty", although, they were less than thrilled with John Thayer's implied threat that if the wedding didn't happen that he would make it his personal mission to basically run them into the ground and make sure that they would never sell another lump of coal again. They decided to just focus on designing the most perfect and unique wedding bands for their only son and his bride-to-be.}

Okay, I have to jump in here for a moment just to move things along. Betty gave birth to "their" one month preemie son and only child, Ben, exactly eight months after the wedding. Ben was the spitting image of his mother so no one even considered that Newtie wasn't the father. It was when Ben was twenty-five and his father needed a kidney that Betty had to tell her long kept secret (never revealing the true identity of Ben's biological father to anyone) because Ben was so adamant about donating one of his to his father. [Note: Eugene Newton Dunnthatt died a couple of years later while on the waiting list for a compatible donor.]

So, obviously when Newtie heard the news that his son WASN'T his son he was outraged and, unbeknownst to ANYONE but his lawyer, he removed his wife from his will. Even though it really didn't make that much of a difference because the medical expenses pretty much "ate up" everything they got from selling Palace Jewelers, it was still a slap in the face to her at "the reading" because he had never divorced her. Another slap in the face to her was that he made Ben the sole heir because he loved his son and knew it wasn't his doing and it put him at ease knowing that it wasn't his genes that made his son "that way". [Note: Again, it didn't amount to much, but still.]

{Ben always knew there was something "different" about himself from the other little boys. He much preferred to play jump rope and hopscotch than dodge ball or kick ball. He also preferred to wear "nice clothes" than jeans and t-shirts. [Note: He never wore or owned a pair of jeans until he was twenty-years-old.] He just didn't know what it was that made him different and prefer to "hang out" with girls and "admire" other boys.

Ben was growing up and his admiration for other boys increased and he knew what the word "gay" meant, but he was desperately afraid of being that so he fought himself and denied and mimicked what society deemed "right". Also, he would have just died if his parents ever found out so he "dated" A LOT of girls. It was going pretty well for him...UNTIL...

senior year in high school a classmate of his, Samuel Daniels, showed up at registration three weeks before the school year started transformed from Summer vacation.}

I gotta jump back in here once again to move it along. Ben and Sam became fast friends at registration, they were always together their senior year, and everyone assumed and speculated and "gossiped" that they were involved (DOING "IT"), but they both dated girls. There was one night, however, before a big weekend trip with all of their friends that something happened that Ben (and Sam, I will explain momentarily) has never gotten out of his mind. [Note: Ryan told me a lot of this while we had coffee and/or breakfast when I dropped off Carlisle in the mornings. That is, on the mornings that Ben wasn't there.] Anyway, for some reason Ben spent the night with Sam before the big trip and, although, nothing sexual happened, there was something in their teenage, raging hormonal angst and "crushes" on each other that happened that night…they "spooned".

So, this is why I said that I'd "explain momentarily" about Sam. He, too, had never gotten that night out of his memory and a few years after the death of his long time partner he, on a whim, decided to look for and found Ben on an internet site to locate former high school classmates. Suffice it to say Sam found Ben. They corresponded a couple of times before they started talking on the phone for a few weeks and then Sam decided, on another whim, to return to Whopping, after being a world traveler, for a visit to "see" his old friend Ben and they connected and Sam, after returning to wherever "home" was for a week, moved back to Whopping and he and Ben are now living their lives together.

Okay, before I go on I gotta quickly tell you a little about both Ben and Sam. Ben is 35, 5'11", around about 160 pounds, dark brown hair, incredibly white teeth, and clean shaven. Sam is 35, 5'7", approximately 145 pounds, longish and reddish hair but graying at the temples, and with a very white/grey goatee. I'll admit I was a little surprised because, and I won't say it is always the case, but I have noticed that gay men seem to be attracted to men who look similar to themselves and that's why I figured Ben was attracted to Ryan and why I was a little surprised that Ben and Sam hooked up. [Note: Again, Ryan didn't seem particularly hurt when his affair with Ben ended.]

Anyway, back to where I was about the Christmas party. I had my elf (so did Ben, and I'm only saying this again because both he and Ryan thanked me PROFUSELY, like I had anything to do with it, while they were seeing each other), but I still needed my Santa and Mrs. Claus. So, my first and REALLY ONLY choices were Kurt and Lana. Unfortunately, Lana couldn't accept because she was headed to Shrewesburg with her son Lucas to spend Christmas with her daughter, son-in-law, and grandchildren, The Bells, and that curmudgeonly old bastard Kurt just flat out refused. [Note: I'll admit that I was somewhat...NO! I was REALLY ticked off at him for not doing it after I gave my time and efforts to him during Thanksgiving! Only for a minute, though, then I just accepted him for who he is and got over it.]

Okay, moving on. I'm not proud. I'll admit that I was kvetching over my dilemma to anyone and everyone who would listen. And THAT'S WHEN two "unlikely parties" offered to take on the roles. Jim Traynor offered to play Santa and Tatiana offered to play Mrs. Claus. [Two notes: I figuratively sank to my knees, clasped my hands under my chin, looked to the Heavens, and said, "Hallelujah," as each one offered and literally sank to my knees and thanked each profusely!] So, I bought Jim a Santa outfit, but Ryan INSISTED that he make Tatiana's Mrs. Claus outfit so she could show off her "assets". All I will say is that she accepted his offer (so did I – with my fingers crossed) and he did and it did and it was tasteful, too. (Thank You, Jesus!) I just cannot stress enough how VERY ARTISTIC the boy is!

Now, there was another hook-up that I totally didn't see coming from all of this. I am, however, delighted and RELIEVED. No, it wasn't Jim and Tatiana, although Jim was one of the parties. The other party, however, was Constance. Yes, Constance. That's why I say I was relieved. After that night Constance Mattering pretty much had forgotten about trying to "land" me.

Oh! I forgot! Well, almost, anyway. Innig accepted Makker's marriage proposal! And I accepted my friend's Best Man proposal when Carlisle and I journeyed home to spend Christmas Eve and Christmas day with them and Camarada and Leslie. [Notes: Innig is a beautiful, brilliant, accomplished, and amazing woman. My certain skepticism about the reason she accepted Makker's proposal so quickly was allayed; I could tell from her eyes the moment I met her that she truly was in love with him. Makker did bring this up to me and we discussed it because he does know me all too well. And I did regale my friends with some stories of the people I'd met and admitted that I was teaching (How could I not?), but again held firm my ground and didn't tell them where Carlisle and I were staying.] All in all I'd say that everyone had a Merry Christmas.

Ringing In

Everyone was getting excited about the annual New Year's Eve "gala" hosted by the woman who had been M.I.A. since my arrival. If you'll remember, she'd been away taking care of a sick relative. Anyway, the relative, some multiple-times removed cousin, had recovered and the absentee resident, Hyacinth Preestiss, was returning. (Convenient?) I do have to admit that even being new and never having the chance to attend the gala nor having ever met Hyacinth ("Hy" to everyone), I, too, was pretty excited. Even with the tragedy that befell two days after Christmas.

I'm not going to beat around the bush. Lana was killed by a drunk driver just a few minutes after leaving her daughter and son-in-law's house in Shrewesburg to return home to Obscurity. Okay, I should clarify. She wasn't killed immediately. She died two weeks later in the S.I.C.U. (Surgical Intensive Care Unit) at Shrewesburg University Hospital in accordance to the terms set forth in her Living Will. [Note: The driver of the vehicle survived, but his three friends in the car with him did not.]

Okay, so, again if you'll remember, she and her son Lucas had gone together, but it was decided that he'd stay through The First and then take a bus home. Of course, Lana being who she was, after just having gotten on the interstate decided to get off at the next exit and go back to give Lucas bus fare so as not to burden his sister's family with the expense. This obviously wasn't necessary, but to Lana it was.

Anyway, a speeding convertible going the wrong way on the exit ramp met Lana's car. It took about five hours to extract her from it. The driver of the convertible walked away with only a few minor cuts and bruises. His three UNseat-belted, fellow Shrewe U student friends were ejected from the UNtopped vehicle. [Note: I know this is very cut and dry and to the point, but TRUST ME it needs to be or you would be bombarded with about three hours of explicit adjectives.]

So, moving on because I really need to, I was saying that despite the tragedy I was still looking forward to the New Year's Eve party. You probably now think I'm some callous and uncaring person. I again allow you to think however you wish, but I am quite the opposite and in my defense, without being defensive, I'll defend myself. Unless you've been faced with the certain demise of a loved one, you don't know it at the time, but when you are trying to convince the said loved one, conscious or not, that they are going to be alright, you are in fact trying to convince YOURSELF and in so doing you try to look forward to things so you don't have to think about the reality of the other situation. And that's why I was looking forward to the party and also finally meeting Hy Preestiss.

{Daisy, Fern, and Hyacinth were the identical triplet daughters born in that order and seventeen minutes apart to Mayor Gardener Stromeirea and his wife Alice four-and-a-half months after his election. [Note: Hy will be the first to say that her father and his campaign committee DID NOT play up the "family values" aspect (obviously BEFORE that became "core" to more recent political campaigns) to get elected.]

The "Stroplets" [Note: Just in case; STROmeirea/triPLETS.] as they were referred to, although no one takes credit for coining them that, were absolutely identical in every way, inseparable, and admired by all in Obscurity during their father's "meteoric" (by Obscurity standards, anyway) political rise through county, state, and federal elected offices. It was during the latter part of the meteoric ascent that the Stroplets developed their own personalities, looks, and identities and moved off in their own directions.}

Okay, quick backgrounds. Daisy, the ambitious, at age nineteen married a first term Mississippi Congressman, Carl Kilgore (some referred to him as "K"ongressman "K"arl "K"ilgore, but she ignored those allegations), and then divorced him three years later when certain of his "affiliations" began to drag HER good name through the mud. Two years later she married Raleigh Mayes, a lobbyist [Note: I'm not sure what he lobbied against/for then.], and they now continue their current and definitely winning anti-smoking campaign using their thirty-four-year-old daughter Virginia and their thirty-three-year-old son Winston as the "poster children" for the affects of smoking during pregnancy.

Fern, the hippy, and her "soul mate" Huan Durrer, a Japanese-American man ten-years her senior, travel the globe helping "communities" plagued with hunger and strife. [Notes: They met when she was twenty and they've never married in the forty years they've been together, however, they are considered "Husband and Wife" by several tribes around the world. They have no children of their own.]

And that brings me to Hy.

{Hyacinth became an invisible behind-the-scenes fixture for her father, his personal assistant, for ten years after her sisters blossomed into individuals and began their lives. She convinced herself that her father's dependence on her (yes, she knew deep down that it was the other way around) was more important than her appearance and she took less and less time on herself and put on weight, not to the point of obesity though, and let her full-bodied, naturally golden-highlighted, lustrous sandy-brown locks become flat, drab, and greasy-looking dirt-brown strings always cut straight across and just above her shoulder blades. [Note: With BANGS no less!]

It was on her thirtieth birthday after she picked up her father's dry cleaning and while she was getting ready to choke down her self-celebratory birthday lunch consisting of a particularly large sized double-cheeseburger with extra everything, large fry, dessert, and large diet drink at a D.C. fast food restaurant that she encountered the porter after she picked up her tray and turned slowly around, she was still carrying her father's dry cleaning, only to step on the white cotton mop being used by him as he was cleaning up a wet spill only then to find herself sitting on the floor drenched in her soda and covered in greasy fries and crying uncontrollably.

It was about an hour-and-a-half later when she returned to the dry cleaners, still soda and grease stained, to return her father's suits for re-cleaning that she met twenty-three-year-old Porter Lee Preestiss, the porter who had been fired on the spot for his customer safety negligence. She walked up to and slapped down on the counter the two dollars and fifty cents that he was promising the woman behind the counter he'd be back with in a few days as he begged and pleaded for his clothes.

Hyacinth spent her next two weeks' lunch breaks meeting Porter Lee as he looked for work and found out that he was in D.C. trying to get his foot in the door of the "political machine" while working ANYTHING just to keep his head afloat because he'd just up and left his life on the farm after earning his Political Administration degree, which was going to waste, the year earlier. Two days later Porter Lee Preestiss joined the team behind Congressman Gardener Stromeirea and three years later, during which time Hyacinth became Mrs. Porter Lee Preestiss, his efforts helped make Senator Gardener Stromeirea.

Hyacinth knew after television's success for JFK over Nixon that Porter Lee would never move beyond being a clog in someone else's machine and her "never told to anyone" dreams of being some sort of high priestess would never come true if they remained in D.C., so, she got an idea for her equally drab, portly, and five-foot-six-inch husband. She had to mix hers and his visions and push him in the direction that she so rightfully deserved. And there was no better place to do that than in Obscurity.

If nothing else Hyacinth had learned two things from being her father's "bitch" for ten years; how to MOVE UP the political ladder and PATIENCE. She became quite the success at "climbing" and of being "patiently impatient" because it took a few years for her to get her husband acclimated, well-introduced, and trusted in Obscurity, but she did and then she became Mrs. Mayor Porter Lee Preestiss.}

Okay, so, I'm going to jump back in here. I know. Big surprise! What I learned from Lana before…well, the accident…is that Mayor and Mrs. Preestiss did more for Obscurity than any other city leader, past or present (her father included), and even though they both were "a little rough around the edges" and may have had "personal gain motives" for what they set out to accomplish, they are and will always be revered, Porter Lee posthumously though, because they did those things for the residents, too.

Before I continue, I should tell you that Porter Lee died from a heart attack when he exerted himself with the "first shoveling" at the ground breaking ceremony for the new community of Obscurity Heights. Also, there are no Porter Jr.'s or Porter-ettes because Hy actually had an affair with a very high ranking government official in her early twenties that led to a pregnancy…and then an abortion that left her sterile. [Note: To my knowledge only four people know about Hy's affair/abortion; Hy, the high ranking government official, Lana, and me…and I've been SWORN TO SECRECY by Lana!]

Now, I have to say that what Lana told me about Hy Preestiss being selfless (even though I was told that she did it in a selfish way mostly) was, IS, true. And I know this because during that week-and-a-half of the New Year that Lana was in the S.I.C.U., Hy was always there helping with and coordinating the influx of visitors in any way she could and I got to know her pretty well while Carlisle and I stayed at a hotel in Shrewesburg so I could visit as often as possible while I was still on Christmas break. Also, Hy was the only non-medical person present when Lana's Living Will wishes were carried out.

Okay, as weird and as bad as this sounds I do have to mention that the New Year's Eve gala was quite the event. And I do this because I hate to leave a story untold. I also do this because Hy did say at the party that Lana would have wanted it that way and having gotten to know Lana as well as I did I have to agree.

Being Bombarded

Lana's open casket (I was surprised that it was, but she looked stunning and she would have been so pleased) funeral was held the Saturday following her death (I know a lot of people prefer to use terms like "passing", but...). It was held at her church, of course, and the turn out was amazing as weird as that sounds. I'm pretty sure all of Obscurity was there, along with family and friends from Whopping and Gross County and even her oldest son Lawrence Jr. flew in from wherever he was on business.

In a nutshell, the church's pastor started off the (I want to say "event", but...) service, then there were several heart-rending remembrances (yours truly gave one, too) intermixed with her favorite hymns and prayers, followed by Lawrence Jr., Lucas, John Bell (her son-in-law), Eddie-Os, me, and, believe it or not, Kurt Mudgeon as pall bearers and, of course, ending with Lana being lowered into the ground of the plot next to her husband.

Now, I've quickly got to tell you why I told you all of that "in a nutshell". You see, even though I was obviously PHYSICALLY there, I wasn't completely MENTALLY there. It may be hard to believe but Lana's was only the second funeral I'd ever been to in my life. I'm not saying I haven't known people who have died during my lifetime, but I wasn't close to them or wasn't close to them at the time they died, that is except for my Lois, and that's why I wasn't completely mentally at Lana's funeral because my mind kept taking me back to Lois and our life together.

{M.E. was twenty-one, attending his local community college part-time in the evenings for a business degree, and working full-time during the days in the gift shop of a very large "Aquarium" tourist spot in the city where he had spent his whole life when one day on his lunch break while sitting and eating at his favorite exhibit he noticed the new tour guide with her short and somewhat wild pinkish-reddish-tinted hair that stood out even more in contrast to the drab uniform consisting of grey pants,

54

navy blazer, white shirt, and one of those horrid, striped, scarf/kerchief neck things that some places make women wear so they appear more business-like.

M.E. was instantly captivated, however, he was very shy (and a TOTAL NERD) and he couldn't just walk up and start talking to her so he did what any "normal person" under those circumstances would do. He found out her schedule and the route of the tour and where she'd be at any given time during the tour and always just happen to be having lunch wherever it was that she'd be when he was on his lunch break.}

Now, I'm going to jump in for a moment to tell you, or NOT tell you as the case may be for reasons I cannot explain because I really don't know why other than possibly to keep my anonymity (that's what I'm going with, anyway). I am not going to tell you my real name, but I will tell you that M.E. are my initials. [Note: I think that makes sense.] Anyway, I am Ryder Autumns and I am M.E. I am me, the writer of tomes.

Oh, I guess I should also tell you that during my three weeks of "stalking" the new tour guide (Lois constantly teased me of that during our life together...while I maintained my innocence), I was able to find out that her name was Lois Engel, she was twenty-four, unmarried but in an on-again-off-again-semi-serious relationship, and was a licensed massage therapist, although why she wasn't using it at the time I still don't know because she never 'fessed up. Anyway, I also somehow managed to learn which car was hers and where she lived, but I never did anything with that information.

{Lois Engel was just ending her first tour of the day with a group of Swedes visiting the States. As usual she took her group into the gift shop as required in her job description, but on a whim she did something "unusual". She took the entire group up to the counter to see the Skunk Fish. [Note: She was being funny because she always referred to people who acted weird as being "skunks", I guess it was an upbringing thing, and she'd been noticing me acting weird for the previous three weeks and there is such a thing as a Skunk Fish and we did work in an aquarium.] What she didn't expect was for the group to start screaming and running.

Lois and M.E. found out in the General Manager's office after the "Near International Incident" why the Swedish tour group became so frightened. Several of the group's members misheard "skunk" as "skurk" which in Swedish translates to "bad guy" which can be loosely translated to "bandit" which among other things translates into "gunman". That's what they were told right before they were both fired, anyway.

After Lois and M.E. were escorted by security officers from the manager's office to the respective women's and men's employee locker rooms to change out of their uniforms and retrieve their personal belongings, they were escorted individually out to the employee parking area. M.E., having taken several minutes longer, saw Lois leaning back against her closed driver's door with her arms up and crossed over her face. M.E.'s "anger" took over and he marched right over to her to give her a piece of his mind and a stern talking to as to what the heck she had been thinking!

Lois dropped her arms down to her sides and just laughed at M.E. She pushed herself from her car and grabbed him by the hand that he was waving at her and told him to shut up and give her a ride home because her battery was dead because she had left her lights on because it had been overcast and raining when she left her apartment that morning. He did as he was told and probably would have gotten away with knowing so much about her, but he drove her home without asking for directions as they comfortably laughed and talked about the whole stupidity and absurdity of the incident that they were fired for.

Lois didn't mention the fact that she didn't have to give M.E. directions and invited me up to her apartment for lunch since it was right about that time. She poured us a drink and then another and another as she made a smorgasbord meal from leftovers in her fridge as I sat at the counter in her...}

WOW! I just realized that I went from a third person account to using first person. I guess that's understandable so I will just stop using flashback-mode to finish telling you about Lois and me and just tell you. We made love that afternoon...and that night...and the next morning.

Now, I'm not normally one to tell my personal business, but I guess that I have to tell because it is pertinent to let you know why I've progressed to my illness. See, although I'd had "intimate moments" with other girls during my high school and college years, I'd never actually "gone all the way". I'm not saying that I was in love with Lois because she was the first woman I ever fu...made love to, but she was the first woman I ever really wanted to make love to. And REPEATEDLY!

Anyway, after skulking home late the next morning (yes, I was worried my neighbors would be able to tell what I'd been up to seeing how I was in rumpled clothes from the day before and UNshowered and smelling of sex - I kind of felt like the male Gilda Radner in that *Saturday Night Live* commercial parody of a perfume called, "Hey, You: The perfume for one night stands"; I don't know if you know it, but she looked pretty bad and VERY VERY FUNNY as it was an *SNL* parody and she was Gilda Radner), I immediately called Camarada and told her I'd just met the woman that I was going to spend the rest of my life with. Three weeks later Lois broke her lease and moved into my apartment with me.

Our cohabitation was great for all of the obvious reasons, but it was also good because I hadn't been able to find a job at that point and she had. She had called up an old friend, Arye Olla, and gotten a job at his tattoo and piercing parlor as a piercing specialist or whatever the hell they are called. Anyway, Arye was gracious enough to hire me on as a cashier/appointment maker/greeter/receptionist/gopher/janitor/anything-else-he-needed-or-could-think-of, too, and I will say that he did try to teach me his craft of tattooing and Lois hers of piercing, but I didn't quite have the stomach for either. [Note: Lois did really try to get me to get a nipple pierced because she found that sort of thing particularly sexy, but I didn't have the stomach for that either...however, she did talk me into and hold my hand while I let Arye tattoo M.E + L.E. surrounded by a heart on a spot on my upper, inner left thigh that she was particularly fond of kissing...I will say that I was particularly fond of kissing her in that same spot, too... OKAY! 'Nuff said!]

So, where the hell was I? Oh yeah, our cohabitation and the new jobs. Lois was quite the hit at Arye Olla's Tattoos and Piercings and brought in a pretty good income and let me quit working (I'm pretty sure Arye talked her into it...and I'm okay with that) while I continued toward my business degree at the community college. Anyway, since I was finally able to go full-time, and to move this along, I got my degree a year-and-a-half later and got an assistant manager position at a local branch of a national book seller retail chain. [Note: This wasn't Makker's, of course, but I met him there as a "customer" about five years later when he was ready to open his own bookstore and he talked me into leaving and going to work for him.]

So, it was during the time that I was assistant manager at the national book chain that I convinced Lois to leave Arye's and start using her massage therapist license. It's not that I disliked Arye or was jealous of her popularity with the young "clientele", both male AND female, of whom I got very detailed descriptions from her almost on a daily basis of the bodily locations that they were having pierced (I don't even know WHAT to say about the sizes and shapes of a lot of those bodily locations), I just knew it was time for her to move on.

I saw an ad in the paper for a massage therapist at a local day spa catering to a somewhat exclusive...well, older, "established" female clientele and it just seemed...are you buying any of this? Yeah, I didn't think so. I'm not really convincing myself either. Not NOW, anyway. I did convince myself then, of course, but I know I was jealous and that's why I convinced her to move on. And God love her because she did for me and...I MISS HER SO MUCH! Anyway, let me quickly "time line" what you already know from there; after Lois started at the spa our two incomes afforded us the condo and then shortly thereafter is when Carlisle joined our happy little family.

Okay, so I've got to keep moving on with this before I can't and I'm not going to go into the whole "medical-ese" of Ovarian Cancer. [Note: There are plenty of websites, etcetera to check out if you need or want to.] What I will say is that her cancer metastasized (spread to other organs in her body) and her five-foot-six-and-a-half-inch one-hundred-and-thirty-two-pound (that's what it started at, anyway) frame, along with her obstinacy put up one hell of a fight not only through the cancer, but the treatment, too, as long as it could.

Now, I've already mentioned it, but my therapy during taking care of Lois' needs and keeping the house and taking care of Carlisle and working, too, was to start writing the novel that I'd been talking about for years. [Note to Makker: Thank you, my friend. I think it's the one thing that helped me to keep my sanity.] I'm just sorry that Lois never got to see it finished and/or in book form. And like I've said, I've written a couple others, too, but they were inspired by things I'd encountered since her death and I have one about ninety-percent done that I actually started after the first one, but I've just never gotten myself to finish it...it's the unabridged version of Lois and my life together...that is, everything up to the funeral.

Oh, God! The funeral! Lana's funeral, that is. That's what I was talking about before I went off on my tangent. [Note: I'm so glad to be back to my original point because frankly I'm TOTALLY – emotionally, mentally, AND physically – EXHAUSTED from thinking about Lois.] Actually, where I was headed was what I found out AFTER Lana's funeral. There were two things.

First, I was asked to be present during the reading of her will. I didn't pay too much attention during the breakdown of distribution of her monetary assets to her children, grandchildren, church, and charities, although I was wondering what she thought she was doing leaving me money when the lawyer disclosed a distribution of funds to Eddie-Os, so naturally I was next. I wasn't. So, I couldn't possibly imagine why I'd been asked to be present as the lawyer went through absolutely everything and I hadn't been mentioned nor thought I should. Cutting to the chase, it was saved till last and Lana left me her house. I was dumbfounded.

Oh, if that was dumbfounding enough for me, there's the second thing. After "the reading" was done and everyone was headed back to Lana's (Whoops…My) house where Lawrence Jr. was staying for a couple of days to make sure everything got taken care of and was in order, Lana's attorney detained me for a little while longer. Long story short, I had to sign some paperwork to make the house and property legally mine. All of that, however, was preceded with a letter from Lana explaining why she left the house to me. To M.E.! She knew who I really was! And according to her letter almost from my arrival.

Okay, I'm not going to keep you in the dark. Without thinking I wrote a check and signed my real name instead of Ryder Autumns. It wasn't a rent check; Aggie had paid that, utilities included, for the whole school year in one lump sum from my Ryder Autumns' account before I even arrived in Obscurity. It was on the second Saturday that Eddie-Os came over to do yard work and Lana had had to go to Shrewesburg at the last minute to her daughter and son-in-law's to watch her grandkids while they went out of town for a wedding and I paid Eddie with a check. Anyway, he noticed the different signature and instead of telling me he took it to Lana to warn her about me, but she put him at ease and paid him and deposited the check so I wouldn't get to wondering why and blah, blah, blah. It was all in the letter.

What else was in the letter was why she left me the house. She said she knew from that first night that we had dinner together till two in the morning and became kindred spirits that I'd been lost for so many years and that over the course of the next few weeks she could tell that I was at home in Obscurity and wherever I was geographically AND in my life when her will was put into effect that I would always have a home, a "safe haven" have you, to come to. [Note: God love her!]

Saying Vows

Before I go on, I have to add a DISCLAIMER (of such, anyway) here. You may have noticed a few "misrepresentations" in my recount. The one that stands out most to me is: *Oh, as I said earlier, it was after this that my dinners with Tatiana began. Actually they weren't always just the two of us, although the majority of them were, but sometimes Ryan and/or Lana would go or one of them would host the rest of us.* I have to say that they (again, this one in particular) are intentional because I need you to experience what I experienced in the order that I experienced them. [Note: How could I have said at the time, "...but sometimes Ryan and/or Lana <u>only briefly</u> would go...", and then not explained WHY it was ONLY BRIEFLY?] Okay, I feel better now.

So, it took me a couple of weeks to get up the gumption to move into the main...my house. The first few days because Lawrence Jr. was there to tie up things with Lana's attorney and for him, Lisanne, and Lucas to retrieve any and all articles of sentimental or monetary value. From what I could tell they pretty much only took photos and such for themselves (Lisanne, mostly) and donated all clothes, jewelry, and things of "real" value to Lana's church to be liquidated however it chose to do so. They left almost all of the furniture, linens, etcetera for me to do with as I pleased. [Note: I'm still to this day not sure if I'm surprised that there was no contest to this part of Lana's will, but I guess after hearing about the story of Lana making her family basically empty out the entire house when they were kids to take everything to Eddie-Os and clan I'm not.]

Well, it obviously didn't take me and Carlisle TOO long to get moved in...or over...or whatever, but I'm glad we did when we did because February became quite the busy little month for us. Okay, really only for me. [Note: Carlisle did spend a couple of busy days constantly searching for Lana since her smell was all over everything, but he did get acclimated, although I could tell that there was a sadness in his eyes from then on, somewhat anyway…Okay, mine, too!] Anyway, I never thought about it before, but I had just been to a funeral, so I guess it was only appropriate that I had three weddings to go to, too. [Note: I do know that that movie's title was actually *Four Weddings and a Funeral*, but, hey, work with me here.]

Okay, one wedding was Makker and Innig's which shouldn't come as a surprise since, as I said earlier, I had accepted Makker's Best Man proposal during my Christmas sojourn home, but I'll save that one for last. Now, neither of the other two should be all that surprising either, but the "announcements" and "invitations" did come kind of last minute so there was an ELEMENT of surprise. I guess the LEAST surprising of those other two weddings was Constance and Jim's. It was less a "wedding" and more a "formality" which was really the true surprise, but I'm going to tell about all three in the order that they happened. And that leads me, of course, to the most surprising wedding…a Commitment Ceremony.

Now, I know you are probably thinking that the ceremony was for my friends Camarada and Leslie, but it wasn't. It was for my colleague Ben Dunnthatt and his lover Sam Daniels. And THAT really isn't the "surprising" part. What surprised me most is that Ryan agreed to throw it together for his former, although brief, boyfriend! The next big surprise was that Ryan asked me to hold it in the backyard of my newly acquired house which is why I was glad that I got moved out of the garage apartment and into the house when I did. [Note: He gave me some bullshit story about not being able to use his house and I pretended to buy it.]

Okay, I hate to say it, but my first thought before I said, and please again pardon my French, "Fuck it," and agreed to play host was, "Oh my God! A GAY wedding? What will the neighbors think?" This was instantaneously followed by the thought that Lois and Lana would storm into God's office, ignore His secretary telling them that The Almighty was in a meeting and couldn't be interrupted, burst through the white double-doors with the gold door knobs, and insist that He immediately drop everything and send down a bolt of lightning onto my head. That is, of course, when I laughed and used my expletive. [Note: I didn't explain all of that to Ryan. After he asked he just saw me pause, laugh out loud, and then cuss. He was nice enough to just ignore it…to my face, anyway!]

Anyway, Ryan told me just a week before that the ceremony was on Sunday, February 1 at ten o'clock in the morning to be followed by a champagne buffet brunch and that I didn't have to do anything except make sure Eddie-Os came by on Saturday to mow, trim, and hedge before the workmen got there at noon to start setting up the tents, etcetera. Alright, let me cut to the chase. Was I nervous? How do I answer that? Oh! All I could picture in my head for a week was the episode of *Roseanne* where Roseanne put the gay wedding on for her business partner Leon and his lover Scott. Also, Ryan got the gay boy band, The Tighty Whiteys, as musical entertainment and I, of course, could only picture a bunch of young boys singing and dancing around in nothing but their skivvies and I don't mean that in the way that it sounds and could be interpreted and now I'm rambling and that's how nervous I was. Okay, I'm just shutting up and moving on.

So, YET AGAIN Ryan was tasteful (I don't know why I kept doubting him, but I've never EVER doubted him again after that day) and put together "quite the lovely affair" as all of the guests kept saying. And they, all, were right! It was QUITE lovely! Two very large white tents, one for the ceremony and one for the reception, were put up next to each other with a "doorway" in between in case of inclement weather and for privacy for the twenty-four guests which included the two "grooms", their church's minister (I'm not much of a gambling man but I'd put money on her being a lesbian), Ryan, me, my "date" Tatiana (yeah, I know, but, again, don't hate), the five Tighty Whiteys, and thirteen more people I didn't know (but obviously now do; some of whom I've seen on occasion since). [Note: The Tighty Whiteys may have been wearing them, but I'll never know because they WERE dressed. There's another "Duh" for me!]

Okay, the "T-shirts to Tiaras" standing only ceremony (in this case SWEATSHIRTS to tiaras…it was February after all) began in one tent after everyone, including the grooms, was served their second glass of champagne during the mingling and ended twenty-five minutes later with a toast to the happy couple. [Note: Ryan and The Tighty Whiteys even being under age for drinking legally had champagne, too. After all it was a private affair.] At the reception there were four round tables that sat six each, two heavily ladened buffet tables that just had everything a carnivore OR a vegetarian could ever want to eat, of course the champagne flowed, and there were several dessert choices to meet the needs of everyone's dietary choices. [Note: I sampled quite a bit of just about EVERYTHING and knew I'd have to do a bit more treadmill.] Afterwards, back in the first tent, The Tighty Whiteys put on quite the "concert" for the Dancing Queens. [Note: I say that with RESPECT and I WAS ONE that day! Although I'm quite sure everyone else would say I was a dancing FOOL!]

Alrighty, I've got to move this along. I wish I had some brilliant storytelling segue into the next wedding that came along, but, alas, I don't. So I'm just going right to it. I said that I wasn't surprised that Constance and Jim tied the knot and really I wasn't. They had been pretty inseparable since the faculty Christmas party. It was the announcement, invitation, and location that took me by surprise. The announcement and invitation happened within about a fifteen minute time period (I give kudos to Constance for actually keeping something brief...for her, anyway) and the location was NOT AT ALL what I expected.

It was Monday, February 9 about ten minutes after my morning Creative Writing class was over when Constance came charging into my classroom to tell me, "Jim proposed to me yesterday morning over coffee and onion bagels with cream cheese and don't you just love the ring he gave me I do it's not too flashy or ostentatious but still quite dazzling and beautiful and I hope he didn't spend too much money because etiquette states that an engagement ring should only be the price of two month's salary and I'm going to go have it appraised for insurance purposes ONLY and NOT to find out how much he spent OR to find out how much he makes in two months and we were up late watching a movie we rented the night before some psychological thriller direct to DVD starring some actor I've seen before but can't for the life of me remember his name because they were only minor roles probably but it was very good and if you want to borrow it you can because it doesn't have to be back for a few days and I was tired and didn't feel like cooking yesterday morning and Jim was okay with it because we had pretty much filled up on popcorn not that the two of us spend many nights together but we are both adults and neither of us are virgins but we had two bags with this tasty seasoned popcorn salt that I found at that new World Grocery Store that just opened a few weeks ago just out off the highway on the way to Gross County and I'd be happy to pick some up for you on my next trip there because I know you live in the other direction and probably won't get over there or better yet I could bring the container I have tomorrow if you aren't a germophobe and I'll just get another one the next time I'm there because I'm there at least every other day to get ingredients for my Culinary Arts students and I'm SO glad that I actually have an expense account sort of anyway it is but it isn't from the school so my students can gain the knowledge that I'm so trying to give them and so they can experience new things to take their learned skills to the next level after they get their degrees and become the true culinary artists they so want to be and because the store has just about everything you'd ever want and a ton of stuff you'd never know you wanted because you probably didn't know about them…" (blah, blah, blah) "…and anyway I called Jim just a few minutes ago because I had an idea and thought we should just go ahead and do it and I want to get married on Valentine's Day but Valentine's Day is Saturday and the courthouse is closed on Saturday and there really isn't enough time to plan a big traditional wedding by Friday and I know it is 'Friday the 13th' but there is time to get blood tests done and everything else and NO it doesn't mean anything bad being on 'Friday the 13th' so we'll just do it at the Whopping Courthouse with a Justice of the Peace and we can have our honeymoon on Valentine's Day weekend and that's even better because it will be truly romantic and we'll find some beautiful little bed and breakfast to go to of course that is if Jim can get the time off from the gym…"

Get the gist? Yeah, thought so! Okay, let me wrap this up first by saying, "Yes! I was listening!" [Note: Well, for the most part. I'm not going to lie; Constance did lose me there for a minute.] Anyway, it did take place that following "Friday the 13th" at the courthouse in between our morning and afternoon classes. There was one more surprise. Okay, two. They told me it was casual. I, of course, knowing Constance, didn't go overboard, but I did wear a slightly dressier version of my usual professor-ish blazer, shirt, and tie. The surprise was that Jim was in a navy blue track suit complete with white t-shirt and white gym shoes and Constance was in her usual black mock turtle, black jeans, black socks, and black clogs with some flour smudges thrown on for good measure. Surprise number two was that I was the only attendee aside from the happy couple, judge, and I'm assuming they were the courtroom's bailiff and stenographer. Oh yeah, since we were kind of in a hurry to get back to campus but still had a few minutes, we popped through a drive-thru and they bought lunch before Jim dropped us off and headed back to the gym. [Note: It was actually quite sweet and DEFINITELY quite memorable.]

Again, I have no brilliant storytelling segue. Makker had informed me since Christmas that he and Innig were to be married on Friday, February 27, Innig's parents' anniversary and coincidentally his birthday (I had already arranged to be off from school the entire week prior), in the evening and that the ceremony was going to be formal. [Notes: He did tell me that the vintage 1940's tux with tails that Lois had bought for me early on in our relationship for a New Year's Eve party would be fine. That is, if it still fit. That was followed by his laughter. I didn't tell him that I was saving that for my own "special occasion" that I had started planning, although at that moment somewhat unconsciously. I just laughed with him.]

So, as I said, I met Makker about into my fifth year as assistant manager at the book store. I was building some display for whoever/ whatever the "release du jour" was when he came up to me and started talking about that author. [Note: I REALLY don't remember who it was because over the course of time from then until he asked me to come work for him he talked about so many different authors that I wasn't familiar with other than in name, and not always in name…which makes me wonder again why he asked me to come work for him! Oh well.] We pretty much instantly connected and he always sought me out whenever he came into the store after that.

Oh! It's come back to me why he asked me to come work for him with my "not so" wealth of literary knowledge, but you have to bear with me because unlike the rest of my story I'm probably going to be a tad wordy… ha-ha-ha. I guess it was Lois. No, it wasn't Lois WHY he hired me. It was Lois who shed the light on me why he offered me the job and who told me to go for it while not really knowing anything about the man. I REALLY didn't know ANYTHING about him. Including his name!

Okay, quickly, when he offered me the job and I told Lois that night, she said I had been talking about "that guy" for months and it wasn't often that I connected so easily and expressed a trust in someone (she could just sense it from me whenever I talked about him and said that she sensed from me he felt the same way, too) and we were in a decent enough financial position and I should just throw caution to the wind and take a chance. She also said that it would be a lesson to me to start asking people their names when I met them instead of waiting so long and then feeling embarrassed because I waited so long. [Note: I ate crow and explained myself and asked his name when he came into the store two days later to see what my decision was.]

Two weeks later (I had to give notice…just in case) I went to work for Makker Comity three weeks before his grand opening. It was during this time that I got a crash course in the ability to talk about a wider range of authors and books than the two or three that I tended to stick to because it was a pretty safe bet that I'd enjoy what it was I was about to read. It was during this time also that I got the basics of Makker's past which is really still about all I know to this day because I'm just not a big question asker and I figure people will tell me what they want me to know.

Anyway, Makker is forty-five and has a three-year older half-brother from his father's first marriage and a four-year younger half-sister from his mother's second marriage. His parents weren't together much longer than to conceive and give birth to him. He knows his sister better than his brother because he lived with his mom after his parents divorced, but he's really not that close to either of them. Actually, Lois told me that Makker had told her one time after we had known him for a few years that I was like the brother he never had…and he has a brother. [Note: I've never told Makker that she told me this!] I've met his mother a few times briefly and sporadically when she came by the shop and I've met his father once, even more briefly, about two-and-a-half months after we opened. I've never met his half-siblings.

Needless to say I was looking forward to really meeting all of them at the wedding. I didn't. Other than the bride and groom, it was me, Camarada and Leslie, Innig's assistant, and a few of her colleagues from the university. It was "informal" black tie, meaning we didn't have matching tuxes (of course I already said I wore that vintage tux, so I guess that was redundant), and Innig wore an elegant, strapless, white satin gown with a string of pearls. Oh, her choice of color for the ceremony was a deep rich purple and her assistant/Maid of Honor's dress and Makker's and my ties did match. The small ceremony and full service reception took place in one of the downtown's premier hotel's smaller hall and banquet room.

Creating Diversions

As happy as I was for all of the couples, I have to admit that my illness was getting the better of me and that's when I decided I needed a diversion from it. In all actuality it was several diversions. To start, I had Tatiana and Ryan over for dinner and asked them both to move into the house with me. Ryan agreed immediately although he asked for the above the garage apartment to which I agreed, but it took a few days of coercion from both me and him before Tatiana accepted.

Ryan started moving things over the next morning before I even had a chance to take Carlisle out, let alone walk him halfway around the block to Ryan's, so he said to take some extra time for myself that morning and pop over to The Obscurity Eatery to begin selling the idea of moving in to Tatiana and he'd go down later for lunch and begin his tactical assault. By the weekend Ryan had most of his stuff moved over and so we, along with Eddie-Os, raided Tatiana's apartment on Saturday morning and finished moving her in by evening. Sunday after sleeping in we went back and cleaned up what had been her home for the past twenty-ish years.

It took the first two days to convince Tatiana to take the Master Suite. She said I should have it since it was my house, but I had already moved into one of the larger extra bedrooms when I moved out of the garage apartment. [Note: I just couldn't bear to take Lana's room.] Of course she acquiesced and then it took about a week for her to be convinced that I really truly wanted her to make that room and the house her home and she could do whatever she wanted to any and all of the rooms. It took a few weeks before the house started falling under the influence of her flair (only little things here and there), but it did. Also, Ryan waited until he had the last of his things moved over before informing his "family" that he had vacated the premises but they could still direct deposit his "monthly allowance".

So naturally we all, Carlisle included, fell into a daily routine. This, of course, made me realize that the diversion from my illness that I created was, as all diversions are, temporary and my despair was rearing its ugly little head again. Luckily I was able to mask it with getting ready for final exams. It was during this time that Ryan and Tatiana started inquiring what I was going to do once the school year was over. I'll admit I was starting to wonder, too. And I cannot leave out that Camarada and Leslie, Makker and Innig, and Aggie, too, were starting to question me.

Now, the latter were easier to put off...so to speak, anyway. They all knew that I was a writer so I asked Aggie, since I was near completion of the novel I had been writing, to set up some speaking/signing dates within day driving distances from Obscurity (not in Whopping or Gross Counties because I could be recognized) for four or five weekends following finals. The former were not as easy because I had to come up with something to stay in Obscurity but be away for the weekends and make it believable because they didn't know my true identity. Oh, and I needed to be able to leave Carlisle at home while I was away...which I never did before!

So, what did I come up with to tell Tatiana and Ryan and the rest of interested Obscurity and Whopping residents? Remember I said about telling the truth in a general and vague sort of way that people will jump to their own conclusions and if they ever come back and say that you said this, that, or the other you can counter with what you actually said and subtly let them know that they made up their own mind what that meant? Well, that only works with acquaintances! So, I had to make up something.

I said that I was going to check out some other community colleges and universities that I had applied to and had since my arrival in Obscurity since responded. It seemed to go over pretty well with everyone...except Ryan. He wanted to go with me and said that that way I wouldn't have to leave Carlisle at home because he'd be there at the hotel to take him out if I got stuck late with interviews or anything and, also, he'd enjoy getting away and checking out some other sights and that it made sense because he didn't work. I do think I kind of hurt his feelings when I flat out told him, "No. It's something I need to do by myself." He did, however, along with Tatiana, agree to dog sit during my travels.

Now, except for the drives to and from my signings and the overnight alone stays in hotels, the six weekends (Aggie being Aggie, I'm sure to pump up my ego, told me that no one declined the offer of my appearing and that's why it was a six weekend tour and not just four or five) with a total of fourteen appearances (Aggie booked me every Saturday and Sunday except for the last weekend which was only Saturday with three weekends of two Saturday appearances) went off rather well (I think I generated a lot of interest for my nearly completed "novel in the works" – You're welcome, Aggie) and kept me diverted from my ever growing illness.

Since my final weekend was just two Saturday appearances and no Sunday, I decided as I packed to tell Tatiana and Ryan that I'd be following the same schedule of leaving on Friday morning and returning on Monday afternoon/evening. I also decided, without telling anyone, that I was going to do something for myself on that Sunday since I had the whole day to myself and I packed my vintage tux, too, along with an item that I had secretly purchased one previous weekend away and stored afterward, casually and haphazardly, in the shed. [Note: Luckily I'm a storyteller because I had to come up with an intricate, yet simple, reason off the top of my head for that item being there to tell Eddie-Os because he kept a very sharp inventory and questioned me about it as soon as he saw it. Will I ever learn?]

Okay, so the few remaining days leading up to my last weekend, I was able to finish and "mostly polish" the ending of the novel I'd been working on (deadlines are deadlines whether self-imposed or mandatory) and packaged up the manuscript (I printed out a hard copy instead of e-mailing the attachment) and got it in the mail to Aggie before I left on Friday morning after a very long walk with Carlisle and a quiet (mostly on my part) "good-bye" breakfast with Tatiana and Ryan.

Now, there is good and bad about the end of a book tour. The good is that there is very little preparing to do before because you've been doing it. The bad is that there is very little preparing to do before because you've been doing it…and that leaves your mind open for all the other things you were trying not to think about, but that is good also because I had to prepare for my, as I said before, "special occasion" that was to take place on Sunday. Oh, except for "tying up a loose end" with the twenty-feet (the info I Googled said three feet, but I thought that couldn't be right so I just got what I thought was enough extra to allow for…well, just to allow because, well, twenty feet sounded like more than enough) of rope that I'd bought and stored in the shed that Eddie-Os found, it was really more mental preparation.

Luckily I did have a diversion from the mental preparation. Did you know there are several ways to tie a noose? I sure as hell didn't. I mean, not before I Googled that, too. Anyway, the website I chose showed five ways to tie one. I'm not going to go into all of the ways, but I did have to choose from two of them: "The Gallows Knot" and "The Hangman's Knot" of which the latter is said to be more merciful because it breaks the neck where the former really just does more of a strangling.

I'll be honest, I really could've used Lois' level-headedness (not that she would've ever helped me to devise a device to kill myself) to focus and ground me and help me decide. Anyway, after much over-thinking and deliberation…and because the cartoon-ish picture (followed by the warning: "Never play hangman. It can really kill.") looked more like what I was used to seeing and because it sounded a lot quicker and I really didn't want to be in the midst of my special occasion and re-think it while flailing around and clawing at my neck and the rope as I was gasping for air…I decided upon the latter, The Hangman's Knot. [Notes: It took quite a bit of time and several replays of the on-line video to get it right, but I did get it. Don't you just love the internet?]

There I go, side-tracked, again. Where was I? Oh yeah, the mental preparation. Actually, before I go into that, I do have to say that a few other things went on in my head while I was fussing with that stupid rope. First is that I've always heard that you don't go to Heaven if you kill yourself, but I was going with and hoping that I'd done enough good things in my life for God to over look this "one small indiscretion" because I really wanted to see Lois. Of course I couldn't help think, too, that I might end up in that "public service office" from *Beetlejuice*. And I was also curious about at what point of the process the whole "life flashing before your eyes" happened. [Note: I think these are some very good arguments for having diversions!]

Okay, back to the mental preparation. I guess to begin somewhere with this I'll start with the location. During one of my drives something called out to me to stop and venture away from the roadway and I found this seemingly untouched wooded area surrounding a very small lake/pond/watering hole and the very perfect tree with the very perfect boulder underneath. Well, it was perfect to me and I CERTAINLY wasn't going to do it in my hotel room and have some poor housekeeper find me and ruin her day and possibly scar her for life wondering every time that she entered a room after that if she was going to find…well, you know. Also, there really wasn't anywhere in the room I felt was stable enough to do it.

Okay, I know what you are thinking. SOMEBODY was going to have to eventually find me SOMEWHERE. SOMETIMES, like I said before, a person's got to do SOMETHING totally selfish that doesn't make sense to himself or anyone else and so I completely pushed out of my mind the thought of the young lovers out for a moonlight rendezvous, the hunter with his dog, or the kids playing finding me.

Let me just move on here. Since I had the location and I technically wasn't checking out of my hotel room until Monday morning, I would go to the front desk on Saturday night after my second appearance and let them know I'd be out all day Sunday and then leave very (very) early Monday morning so I'd just like to go ahead and finalize my bill so I could just hit the road when I awoke. [Note: In case I forget when the time comes, they asked if I needed a wake up call. I declined because it made sense to me for not arousing concerns since I wouldn't be there to answer it, even though I know those things ARE automated.]

I guess the last of the mental preparation was (aside from running over in my head a hundred times the mental checklist of noose, tux, location, and checkout procedures to give plenty of time before anyone started looking for me) focusing on and realizing that my illness was finally being cured, but not over-thinking it. [Note: Is it too late for that?] I'm sure that it will come as no surprise that there were a gazillion other things that popped in and out of my head, but I won't go into them. I'm sure I could if I put my mind to it, but I'm at such peace where I'm at now that I just really don't want to cloud my head with all of that.

So, there's not really anywhere to go now but onward. I got up Saturday morning and did my morning regimen, got dressed for my two appearances, went to the lobby for the complimentary breakfast (I wasn't particularly hungry, of course, but thought it best to have a little something in my stomach), went back to my room and double checked for about the eighth time that I had all of my notes and everything else that I'd need, and left an hour before my first appearance at 11 A.M. because I like to be early so I'm on time and because I had a thirty minute drive because Aggie booked me at hotels where they take pets. [Note: All of them don't and I never bothered telling Aggie that Carlisle wasn't accompanying me because I didn't want to raise any suspicions). Oh, I did do one other thing on my way to my appearance. I stopped at a gas station and bought a pack of cigarettes. What the heck! It's not like THEY were going to kill me!

Now, to give you an idea of what a book speaking/signing appearance consists of if you've never been to one, at least one of mine anyway, I start by reading a particularly outrageous excerpt from one of my previously published novels to capture the audiences attention and then segue (much better at appearances than when I'm just rambling) into the whole story and inspirations interspersed with other excerpts as they fit in and flow (carefully and methodically placed). I do this with each of the books and then finale with a little about my current manuscript and give the audience a "first look" reading with an excerpt from it. That all takes about forty to fifty minutes, depending, and then I follow it with a Q&A session which can take anywhere from fifteen minutes to an hour, depending, followed by signing copies of my books. Aggie books me for three hours at every appearance to allow.

The first appearance that day only lasted about two hours so that gave me three hours until my next one. [Note: Aggie gives me two hours in between double booking days to allow time for lunch, driving, and personal stuff.] Now, I'm not going to lie. The very first thing I did…well, the very first thing I did after I got in my car and drove about five minutes down the street from the bookstore and parked in an empty section of a parking lot of another strip mall so no one who'd been at my appearance would see me…was have my first cigarette in about three years. And oh my God it was just the most vile and disgusting thing I'd put in my mouth in, well, years. So after the rush and almost drunken feeling from it subsided, I smoked two more.

Feeling relaxed and still having about two-and-a-half hours till my next appearance which was about twenty-five minutes away, I decided I'd better get myself something to eat because I was feeling hungry and because it might be as late as eight o'clock before I got another chance to get something to eat. I inventoried my surroundings from where I was standing outside my car and decided on a fast food burger and fries place a couple of blocks down the street. It's when I was getting ready to light up another smoke for the drive there that the stink of my newly re-acquired, although obviously temporary, habit overwhelmed my nostrils (I'd totally forgotten about the smell, even though I can smell it on others all the time) and I knew I couldn't go into my next appearance with it radiating from me and since I didn't have a change of clothes…

Now, you can say what you want about the commercialism of our towns and cities (I have), but when it comes right down to it we are all grateful for those areas that are really nothing more than national retail chain meccas. I especially was right at that moment because I needed to buy a bottle of the cologne I wore (I didn't think to bring the one I already had from the hotel because buying the pack of cigarettes was a spur of the moment thing) and I did need the same scent which cannot be purchased just anywhere and also some mouthwash. Oh, and a brush and hairspray for after I ran some cologne through my hair to get the smell out of that, too, and then get it back to my liking. I did luck out. The grocery store across the street from where I sat to have my smokes that I ran into for the mouthwash, brush, and hairspray had a fragrance counter and they happened to carry mine. One stop shopping! Gotta love it!

Alrighty, I guess I should tell you quickly why I stopped smoking in the first place. It wasn't because my doctor (my real doctor, not "Dr. Webster") told me to, or else. No, he actually always asked if I'm sure I did smoke because he never smelled it on me and my lungs never sounded like I was a smoker and even the x-ray that was done of my lungs when I went to start my regular regimen of physicals didn't really show any signs of being a smoker. The incentive to quit was because none of my friends smoked and I always kind of felt like I was putting them out if we went out and did anything and I had to make them wait a few minutes while I had a "quick one". Of course there was the smell on me while I was out with them, even though none of them ever said anything.

Okay, enough about me. Sort of. I should move on to the part about how I hoped God would forgive my indiscretion and let me be with Lois, again. I do have to, however, preface that with telling you about the rest of the day leading up to that. After I left the grocery store with my un-stinking and grooming goods, I grabbed a bite to eat at the fast food joint (I ate inside), drove (and enjoyed a few more cigarettes) to my next speaking/signing engagement, unstunk and groomed myself in the car after another quick one behind the shopping center (I'd like to say that maybe one day I'd get a better place than in my car to "ready" myself for an appearance, but knowing what was happening the next day that seemed improbable), had a great three-and-a-half hour engagement, went back to the hotel and did all of my pre-planned "checking out" at the front desk, and returned to my room (with the six-pack of beer I stopped and bought – and another pack of cigarettes) to mentally prepare myself for my final adventure (?) the next day.

Defining Life

It was about 1:30 A.M. Sunday morning (Saturday night) and I hadn't slept a wink. I may have drifted off slightly once or twice, but for the most part I was awake thinking about what I was about to do while trying NOT to think about it. [Note: I'm sure you have had those moments and know what I'm talking about.] Anyway, I just decided to not put off the inevitable and get my butt up out of bed and get ready to go do what I had so carefully planned.

So, after showering (I didn't need to shave because I had before my appearances and I really truly only need to do it every other day and because…well, you know) I just threw on some jeans and a shirt and some comfortable shoes, packed the tux, my dress shoes that have become my "dress for casual" shoes for appearances (because I totally forgot to pack my shoes that I do wear for dressing up – DAMNIT!), and the twenty-feet of noose/rope up into the ugly and laughable, little, pink-ish/plum-ish colored suitcase that I found in Lana's…I mean, MY closet (not an easy task and it kind of looks like something out of the sixties or seventies – that is, of course, the nineteen-sixties or seventies). After a few minutes of debate of whether or not to take everything else or just leave it (the latter won so the housekeeping staff could divvy it all up as an extra bonus to the cash tip I left – I have a feeling they'd like the four remaining beers the most – I dumped the one that was opened but untouched), I left the key card on the kitchen-ette counter and got into my car for my drive to my perfect spot to do what I had to do.

It was about 5 A.M. and I'd been driving about two-and-a-half hours and I still had about an hour to go because the spot I'd picked was found on my second weekend of appearances and for whatever reason (I chalk it up to never ever having decided before to end my life and I guess because I hadn't eaten anything since my stop at the fast food place before my second appearance and also I wondered if one should eat before they do the final deed and because the drive was kind of long and my stomach WAS grumbling) decided to stop at a little twenty-four hour diner I saw advertised on one of those "gas, food, lodging" highway signs that our country has so felt the need to post to help us on our journeys...no matter what our journeys are.

A few minutes later I was sitting in my car in the parking lot of The Roadway Diner looking through the big plate glass windows amazed that *Alice*'s Mel's Diner existed. Oh, another thought went through my head, too, and I'll just simply say, "The Road-KILL Diner," and let you interpret it as you wish. Okay, by this time not only was my stomach still grumbling, but REGULARITY was kicking in (thank God for regularity, don't even get me started) and I thought it best to just chance it. What's the worst that could happen?

So, after I finished in the facilities I sat down at the counter where the waitress motioned to my awaiting cup of coffee that I ordered upon entering before rushing into the bathroom in case they tried telling me that whole "for customers only" stuff and picked up the menu that was, also, awaiting me. As I was carefully perusing for what was to be my last meal (everything actually sounded good), a couple of guys sat down at the counter with only one seat in-between me and one of them. [Note: Hellooo!?! They could have given the proper and unspoken societal seating distance of three or four seats considering there was no one else at the counter or they could, even better, have sat at one of the many remaining unoccupied booths.] Well, after subtly letting them know my indignation of their total disregard for rules AND my personal space with a rather firm yet casual menu placing on the counter, the waitress came over to me after giving them menus and the sodas they ordered (sodas at five o'clock in the morning?) and took my order of the breakfast special and confirmed my feelings by pretending to not even notice them while taking my order and putting it in the little metal turny-thing in the pass-through to the kitchen before picking up the coffee pot and taking it out to refill the booth customers' cups. [Note: People won't learn unless we teach them!]

Before I could decide my next subtle gesture of indignation, the coffee started working its magic and "Round 2" of regularity distracted me back to the facilities, but not before I asked the waitress a quick question. When I finished I was delighted to see my plates of food and a fresh full cup of coffee waiting on the table at the booth in the corner. I thanked the waitress and ordered a glass of orange juice as I passed her (I have tried in the past to order it with my breakfast and ask for them to wait to bring it with my breakfast, but, well, that's why I wait to order it once my food is brought) and walked by the backs of the two young men (with their similarly buzzed-cut heads) who were obviously too afraid to recognize my triumph.

I was going to sit on the side of the booth with my back to the rest of the restaurant and pull my plates over to me, but I was feeling quite victorious with the last stand I'd ever take at social unjust so I sat where the waitress had put the plates. I even gave one cursory nod to one of the young men during one of their finally brave, few, quick rapid succession glances over at me (they looked like they were watching separate tennis matches) as I voraciously dug into my bounty before me.

What I failed to realize when I made my acknowledgment was that it could be misconstrued as an invitation. It was. The young man, really just a boy barely out of his teens if even, who had been closest to me at the counter got off his stool and walked over to my table in his short-sleeved, white button-down shirt with his skinny black tie, navy blue pants, black sneakers (with white socks, nonetheless - his friend was dressed pretty much the same), and holding what was clearly some sort of bible in his hands in front of him. Just what I needed, a Jehovah's Witness to be my last encounter.

He said in a very comforting way while holding the OFFERING out to me, "Excuse me. I'm sorry to bother you, but is this yours?"

I, of course, responded quickly, "No. I didn't bring anything in with me, but thank you." [Note: My response was followed by the thought that THAT was quite a unique approach!]

He said, "No, I mean did you write this book?" He flipped the book over to the back cover and held it closer to me. He pointed to a picture on it and asked, "Is that you?"

Intrigued and forgetting my last meal as I took the tattered and worn book from him to closer inspect the picture, I laughed first because it was a paperback edition of my very first novel and I couldn't believe I was seeing myself in the goofy picture I used for it, and then said, "Yes, that's me. It's my book. I mean, I wrote it, yes." I turned it all over looking at it and then said, "Where DID you get this from?"

Before he could answer he looked back at his friend at the counter who yelled to him that their food was ready and he looked back at me with an expression like he wanted to say more but didn't know what to say so he just mumbled some apology for bothering me again and I handed his book back to him and he turned and started to walk back.

I said (and I really don't know WHY I said it, but I did), "Hey, would you two like to join me?"

I ended up sitting there and talking with Christian Soljur and DeForrest Fordatries for about two hours. While I answered questions about writing and publishing (Christian, the one who had my book, was an aspiring writer) and told the *CliffsNotes* version of my year in Obscurity (Wow, it was almost a year) and all of the interesting people I had met (I, of course, left out what I was on my way to do), I learned they weren't Jehovah's Witnesses, but locals and freshmen at the nearby Christian college and that Christian was looking to pursue a life with The Church after graduation and DeForrest was going there because it was close to home.

I probably would have sat and talked longer, but the boys had to go because they still had a bit of a bike ride ahead of them and they were going to be late for some mandatory Sunday thing as part of their summer school curriculum (they declined my offer of trying to load their bikes in my car and driving them) and I still had an hour or so to drive before I reached my destination. I did, however, insist on paying for their meals and gave them each a signed copy of the book of their choice (I had a few new hardback copies of each of my books in my trunk in case I'd gotten to a signing and they were low on stock) while we exchanged a few last words and pleasantries in the parking lot before they rode off.

As I just stood watching the boys ride off, Christian Soljur turned his head toward me and yelled, "It's nice to meet someone who knows how lucky they are. Most people can't see the forest for the trees."

So, thank God for "auto-pilot" because I don't even remember that last hour of the drive. I can't even tell you what I was or wasn't thinking about because I have no idea. All I CAN tell you is that when I snapped back into the moment I was sitting in my idling car off the beaten track of the highway (not even sure how long I had been sitting there, although by the dashboard clock probably only a matter of minutes or seconds) and staring at the bend in the little access road that I was about to be trudging along with that ugly and laughable, pink-ish/plum-ish colored suitcase (it bears repeating for the full picture) of accoutrement in hand before heading off of it to my perfect boulder and perfect tree.

I'd be lying if I said I wasn't a tad bit trepidatious. Not really about what I was getting ready to do, but because I'd arrived later than I thought I would and was afraid that there'd be at least one person around if not a lot of persons. And then what would I do? My fears were allayed, however.

There wasn't another two-legged creature about (well, except for some birds here and there, but you know what I mean).

So, after assessing the branches and finding one that looked big and strong enough and was not directly above the boulder from which I was to take my leap, I set my suitcase down (I didn't realize that I was still holding on tight during my assessment), opened it and took out the pre-noosed rope (thank God I had the wherewithal to get twenty feet), slung the looped end around the branch (that took a few tries), and tied the loose end around the trunk of the tree. I then glanced around again before quickly undressing and changing into my vintage tux.

After folding up the clothes I had been wearing (yeah, I know) and putting them in the suitcase and placing it at the base of the tree, I got on top of the boulder and stood for a while just listening to the quiet cacophony of nature. When I was ready to do what I'd come there to do, I had to get off the boulder and find a stick long enough to reach the motionless noose to bring it to me. So much for planning.

Okay, so noose was finally in hand when I was struck with a thought. Just to make sure that the branch was strong enough and that I'd tied the other end around the trunk tight enough, I took the rope in my other hand, too, and took a practice jump swinging out over the water and back a few times. [Note: If anyone had been around, I'm sure just the sight of a man in a tux swinging at the local watering hole would have been enough to call the authorities.] Luckily I somehow managed to get all of that right and swing back far enough to regain my footing.

So, with confidence I put the noose around my neck and tightened it. I realized two things immediately. First, the shirt collar and bow tie were kind of in the way and second, I knew I'd been letting my hair grow out, almost down to my shoulders, but it sure hurts like hell when hairs get tangled into rope and get yanked. Anyway, after a few adjustments I re-tightened the noose and looked out over the water. I was ready.

Right as I was about to enter my own private obscurity I was suddenly struck with another thought. Actually it was several and almost all at once. [Note: Okay, I know now that I'd had this thought before while I was fussing with that rope in the hotel room, but it was different this time.] Suffice it to say they all pretty much had to do with that moment that you hear about when your life flashes before your eyes. I have always assumed (and you know what they say, "Don't assume - it only makes an ASS out of U and ME") that it would happen right before, or as, the last breath of life ebbs out of you. Hhhmmmm, maybe it does.

Obscurity or Bust II

I can't say I'll never know at exactly what moment one's whole life flashes before their eyes or for that matter if it really does. I can't say it because they say, "Never say never," and because I am going to die one day whether it be by someone else's actions or my own (it just wasn't on God's "calendar of events" for that Sunday) and I'll know then one way or the other, but I won't be able to share that information because I don't think real death gets a narrative like in *American Beauty* or countless other movies, good or bad. [Note: Just for the record – the movie I named, in my opinion, was one of the good ones. Very good.]

Anyway, the information I can share (and I'll do so in summary form because I think you'd prefer that as opposed to an actual account of the whole series of "flashes", if you can call them that) is what went through my mind as I was standing there on the edge of that rock in my vintage tux, eyes closed, body rigid, fists clenched (I had some fingernail cuts in my palms for a few days following), noose tightened around my neck, and taking deep and deeper and deeper breaths (yeah, again, I know) getting ready to jump. Oh, before I summarize what went through my mind, right before the flashes I heard Christian Soljur's voice say, "It's nice to meet someone who knows how lucky they are. Most people can't see the forest for the trees."

[Note to God: If we are lucky enough to get a flashback of our life and are even luckier to get a narrative, I'd like to put my request in now for the British guy who narrated *Little Children*.] So, not to keep you in suspense, immediately after I "heard" Christian Soljur, I saw the "Welcome To Obscurity" sign, the business district, Obscurity Heights, Lana running to the car when Carlisle and I first pulled up, Lana in her coffin, Hy's New Year's Eve party, Hy at the hospital after Lana's accident, Tatiana at the eatery, Tatiana moving in, that curmudgeonly old bastard Kurt, Ryan outside his house with Carlisle that first day we met, Ryan at all the events he took me to or planned, gay or not, Ryan's doodles of our names together, Lana, Tatiana, and Ryan in various combinations over the (almost) year, Christmas with Camarada, Leslie, and Makker, meeting Innig, Makker and Innig's wedding, Constance and her flirty lunches at school (all the images of Constance was with her mouth constantly moving), Constance and Jim's quick little wedding, Ben and Sam's ceremony, The Tighty Whiteys (???), the fight with Eddie-Os, the fun with Eddie-Os and Carlisle, and in the midst of the melee of images, happening in no particular order to make any sense whatsoever, Aggie's face popped in there once or twice, too.

Now quickly before I go on, I have to tell you that I wasn't magically or instantaneously over my loss of Lois nor was my despair gone completely. However, even though my outlook DIDN'T take a one-hundred-and-eighty degree turn, I was transformed enough by the flashes to realize that my illness was neither terminal nor debilitating…anymore. I finally saw the forest! So, I guess in a way I DID die that day on that rock.

I must also tell you that, in my experiences, usually with epiphanies comes a sense of urgency to find someone close and share them. Not so much this time. I mean, I did want to share my epiphany, but with someone who I didn't have to really explain the whole "ending my own life" part that came with it. And that's why Carlisle was who I couldn't wait to see, but I didn't feel the need to rush back to my car and go speeding home to see him. Don't get me wrong, I was excited to see him, but I did take the time to change out of my tux and into my other clothes AND pack the tux back into the suitcase. Oh, I did leave the rope (I did undo the noose, however, and quickly tied a series of regular old knots) so that there was something to swing out over and jump into the water for anyone else that might come along (it was pretty fun).

Well, I did take longer than I thought I would to go back home. See, the drive would've only taken just under three hours, but as I said, Tatiana and Ryan thought I was doing interviews and weren't expecting me back until Monday afternoon/evening which means there would be, as Ricky would tell Lucy, "Some 'splainin' to do," and as I said also, I didn't really want to have to do that. So, I checked into a motel in Whopping so I wouldn't have that far to go when the time was right. [Note: I was fully prepared to pay another night's stay just to have a late check out later that Monday afternoon.]

Of course everything was rather uneventful…and boring! Oh, I cannot tell you how bored I got without boring you. I was just so ready to get back home and put everything behind me, but I got a six pack and some smokes, ordered a pizza, and just sat back (okay, I did a lot of pacing and running in and out of the hotel room to smoke) and "watched" television. I was luckily able to doze off a few times which did help pass the time.

Okay, let me try to wrap this bit up as quickly as possible. It was around about 11:30 PM that Sunday night and I was wide awake, wired, and anxious so I decided to just get the hell outta there and make the forty minute drive home. [Note: I guess my decision came also because I was still slightly inebriated from the six pack of beer I drank that didn't get soaked up by eating only one half slice of the large, thick crust Supreme pizza I ordered and I convinced myself that I could just kind of "waltz" in unnoticed.] Anyway, I went ahead and checked out at the desk, made the drive home, parked across the street like that first day I got there, got out of the car, and walked up the drive to go into the house through the kitchen door as quietly as possible.

I did manage to waltz in quietly, but NOT unnoticed. Yes, Carlisle decided to give me a somewhat noisy welcome. He was followed by Ryan who stayed in the house and slept in the living room so Tatiana felt safer (I totally forgot about this) and then, of course, Tatiana came to the kitchen to see what all the commotion was. Even though I was slightly inebriated I wasn't that drunk that I couldn't come up with a quick excuse of being so glad that the last interview was done that I just wanted to come home. They bought it and after about an hour of talking, Tatiana returned to her bedroom and Ryan retired to his home above the garage. Carlisle stayed with me in the kitchen while I fixed myself a REAL drink and putzed around to make myself something to eat before going to bed. I was STARVING!

I was finished with the condiments and veggies part of the sandwich that was already too big for my mouth, let alone my stomach, and decided to make myself another real drink and go sit outside and have a cigarette before I finished it with the mountain of meats and cheeses I'd already pulled out of the fridge. I'd just taken a big relaxing swig of the (more heavily liquored than the first drink) drink and was lighting my cigarette when my attention was drawn to the light coming through the open door of Ryan's and Ryan coming down the steps in nothing but a pair of long, loose baggy shorts.

After adjusting himself to sit, picking up my glass and taking a long drink, and taking a cigarette out of my pack and lighting it, he said, "I'm really happy you decided to come back."

Shocked at his words and trying to feign ignorance at his insight that I didn't know from where it came, I non-chalantly (hopefully) said while looking up at the sky and not at him, "Well, I was going to stay the night at the hotel and come home tomorrow, but it was the last interview and I just wanted to get home tonight."

"I love you, Ryder, but you're full of shit." Ryan put his cigarette in the makeshift ashtray (a cereal bowl I brought out, too, since I didn't have an ashtray), drained the rest of my drink, and stood up with the glass. After opening the door to the kitchen, he said, "I'll make us both one. Be right back."

All I really heard was his admission of his feelings for me that I had felt pretty much from the beginning and that might very well have been the longest three minutes of my life as I sat there until he came back outside, handed me my drink, and sat back down beside me.

After a long drink and lighting a new cigarette, I blurted out my courageous response as I turned to him, "Ryan, I'm really flattered and if I were, well, gay, I would probably be in love with you. No, let me finish," I said quickly as I saw he wanted to say something, "I've known your feelings for me almost since we met when I saw the doodles you made of yours and my names together and, again, I'm really flattered-"

Ryan started laughing and tried to control it which only made him laugh harder.

Obviously I was confused.

Finally Ryan was able to say, "I'm sorry, I don't mean to laugh, but I'm not IN love with you. I DO love you, but like a father."

"What about the way you intertwined our names together and put my last name after your first name?"

Even in the low light I could see Ryan blush before he lowered his head.

Looking back up at me, he said, "Well, you weren't supposed to see that, but I just thought since you were RY-der and I'm RY-an, well, I was just doodling while talking on the phone to a friend one day and, well, my mind wandered. I'm so sorry if I made you think otherwise, but, hey, if I were a straight woman, I'd probably be IN love with you."

After a very brief moment we both had a hardy laugh and finished our drinks.

I picked up our ice-filled glasses and stood up while saying, "You sure it's not more like an older brother? Don't say anything. Just get up here and open the door for me and come in the kitchen and let your old dad teach you how to make a REAL drink."

Ryan got up, opened the door toward him, bowed his head slightly, and passed his other arm in front of himself in the direction of the kitchen.

I stepped up into the kitchen, stopped, turned around (making him almost step right into me), and said, "Just so you know, if I had a son, I wouldn't be more proud than if he were exactly like you," then I kissed him on the forehead and turned around to make us another drink while we finished making that monstrous sandwich I'd already started.

Oh, so as not to leave YOU hanging (no pun intended), I have decided to stay in Obscurity for at least another year (school year, anyway) as "Ryder Autumns" and teach my Creative Writing and Public Speaking classes (hopefully enrollment will pick up to add at least one more class of each) after I return home and spend the rest of Summer Break with Camarada, Leslie, Makker, Innig, and, of course, Carlisle will be going and I've decided to take Ryan. I asked Tatiana to come along, but she declined because that curmudgeonly old bastard is hanging up the apron and selling The Obscurity Eatery and she's buying it. She is taking a week though, before she takes over, to come meet my friends (and, yes, I realize that this means the whole truth about M.E. will be opened to Ryan and Tatiana) and then go with me and Ryan to San Francisco for four days while I do some business with Aggie on the new book. [Notes: Wait! Ryan? San Francisco? God, help me!]